Nexus

A Neo Novel

D1343680

Deborah Morrison
Arvind Singh

Manor House Publishing Inc.

Library and Archives Canada Cataloguing in Publication

Morrison, Deborah
    Nexus: journey to the centre: a novel / Deborah Morrison, Arvind Singh.

ISBN 0-9781070-0-4

    I. Singh, Arvind, 1970- II. Title.
PS8576.O7413N49 2006   C813'.6   C2006-903050-2

Cover illustration: Tom Sardelic: *Falling Petals*
based on a photo by Leah Rose Morrison
Cover design: Sardelic/Morrison/Davie

Copyright 2006: Deborah Morrison and Arvind Singh.
Published October 15, 2006
Manor House Publishing Inc.
www.manor-house.biz
(905) 648-2193
First Edition. 192 pages. All rights reserved.

Printed in Canada.

We gratefully acknowledge the financial support of the Government of Canada through the Book Publishing Industry Development Program (BPIDP), Dept. of Canadian Heritage, for our publishing activities.

We lovingly dedicate this book to our friends and family,
who have helped us along the way. You know who you are.

Manor House Publishing Inc.
www.manor-house.biz
905-648-2193

Foreword

NEXUS is one of the most unusual novels you're ever likely to read – and one of the most spiritually fulfilling and enjoyable.

Written almost entirely in the present tense, and incorporating spiritual teachings and *Mystical Poetry* selections, *NEXUS* follows the soul-searching journeys of an odd mix of people thrown together at a spiritual retreat designed to help them cope with the pain in their lives and overcome their shortcomings to find the centre of their being, the Nexus.

Central character Logan is a stressed-out, suicidal American-Canadian journalist, overwhelmed by a series of losses in his tragic life and beset by visions of a spiritual guru, when he comes upon a chance opportunity to meet up with the guru of his visions.

He soon finds himself on a jet headed for a small town in Canada and realizes he's embarking on a remarkable journey of self-discovery and self-worth that's connected with everyone and everything around him. Yet nightmarish thoughts of suicide return to haunt him.

Can Logan Andrews exorcise inner demons propelling him to self-destruction before it's too late?

Following his vivid dream, Logan is guided to a spiritual retreat where he meets his lost love, Sarah, along with an arrogant millionaire, a grandmotherly woman and two insightful teachers.

Problems soon emerge for Logan and others at the retreat. What happens to each character and the depth of their personal experiences makes *NEXUS* a journey of transformation... and a compelling and captivating read.

- **Michael B. Davie,** *Poetry for the Insane: The Full Mental*

Contents:

Foreword   5
About the Authors   7
Chapter 1:   Escape   11
Chapter 2:   Fated Journey   27
Chapter 3:   Mystery and Enchantment   39
Selections: From *Mystical Poetry*   41
Chapter 4:   Where is Peace?   61
Chapter 5:   Wisdom of the Heart   75
Chapter 6:   The Circle of Life   95
Chapter 7:   Psychic Surgery   115
Chapter 8:   Revelations   131
Chapter 9:   The Nexus Connection   145
Chapter 10: The Turning Point   163
Chapter 11: The Trigger   171
Chapter 12: Transformations   183
Reading List: 190

About the authors:

Deborah Morrison

One of Canada's most insightful writers, **Deborah Morrison** of Hamilton, Ontario, is a poet, novelist and speaker, inspired by the healing power of the written word, nature and people.

An early childhood educator; psychotherapist/counsellor, and yoga instructor, she's used her abilities to foster growth and learning. She holds an Honours degree in Religious Studies/Sociology from McMaster University and has extensively researched Eastern and Western thought within the framework of contemporary and comparative studies.

She's also written several published articles on natural therapies, yoga, psychology and metaphysics.

Morrison is also a distinguished member of the International Society of Poetry with many poems published via the International Library of Poetry. She is also past vice-president of the Tower Poetry Society of Hamilton. *Nexus* is her second book. Morrison is also author of the inspiring *Mystical Poetry,* also published by Manor House, in 2000.

Arvind Singh

Also of Hamilton, **Arvind Singh** is a thoughtful, spiritual, creative individual, who asks the big questions: Why are we here? How do you live a good life? What is real? What is unreal? By delving into these questions, he's found insights to share with readers.

He has an Honours B.A. in History from McMaster University and has researched spirituality and religion from a multi-disciplinary perspective.

Having developed an interest in different cultures; and having grown up in Canada, which welcomes diversity, Singh has found many eclectic sources of wisdom. He's written magazine and newspaper articles in English and South Asian languages and enjoys taking the reader on a journey, using words of inspiration. *Nexus* is his first novel.

Manor House Publishing Inc.
www.manor-house.biz
905-648-2193

Nexus

A Neo Novel

Deborah Morrison
Arvind Singh

Manor House Publishing Inc.

*Compassion is the keen awareness
of the interdependence
of all things.*
-Thomas Merton

1

Escape

Logan rests in his bed, wondering how long it will take for him to die. He had finished the whole container of pills and now he waits. When death comes, will he step into the light like many reported near-death experiences?

Or, will he go into nothingness, a total void? Whatever happens, he feels confident he will be in the same state as before his birth, a non-being state — free from hopelessness, loneliness and despair.

Logan is pleased he decided to push the exit button instead of just contemplating it. His eyes begin to close and his mind clouds with the effects of the drug. He won't have to wait much longer...

Suddenly, a nauseous feeling in the pit of his stomach creates terrible pain he's never felt before, an acidic, burning sensation. He rushes for the bathroom and with his head in the sink; he throws up the contents in his stomach.

To his disappointment, the pain doesn't end – it just gets worse as the burning sensation is now no longer isolated to his stomach but moves up his chest like acid reflux.

Logan didn't plan his death to be painful but the pills had unforeseen consequences. Now he just wants the pain to be over.

He dials emergency and after some time the paramedics are at his door. He feels ashamed of his suicide attempt and even more embarrassed he failed to kill himself.

Logan is rushed to the hospital because the pills are still in his system. One of the paramedics notes: "You know, you're lucky that you vomited when you did but you're still not out of danger. What you've taken is serious stuff and we've got to get it out of you right away."

The next moment, Logan starts feeling faint. Everything becomes a daze. Then complete darkness.

The ambulance attendants wheel him to Emergency on a stretcher with nurses and doctors ready to go into action. They pump his stomach of all its fatal contents by inserting a tube through his mouth. Then the stomach is washed out with some salt water.

Once Logan regains consciousness, the nurses ask him to take an awful-tasting gritty charcoal liquid. He suffers great agony from the terrible salt water still in his intestines and from this charcoal now going down his throat.

At the moment, he avows to either change his heavy consciousness through some sort of transformation, or to make sure that his next attempt is more effective in doing the job, with something more violent.

He doesn't like a painful option but he can't fail again because he doesn't want to again go through the ordeal of having his stomach pumped, swallowing the nauseating salt water and tasting the gritting charcoal. It's much better to die, he reasons, than to undergo all that. His whole experience makes him nauseous and light-headed. Soon his mind grows weary with one final thought: "What's wrong with me?" Then, he drifts to sleep…

Logan has what many people would envy: While only in his mid twenties he has achieved stability, living in a quiet cottage near scenic Cypress woods in Northern California with a successful career as a journalist. Yet, despite all that, he feels lonely and disconnected.

Logan's depression worries him because he is unable to move on with life. The next morning, he doubts that he could survive another crash. He despairs: *I don't have any hope of getting better. Even the anti-depressants I'm on haven't helped.* His thoughts are broken as he hears footsteps approaching his room.

Dr. Elizabeth Knight, a psychologist, enters the room carefully looking at his chart. At length, she speaks: "Well, Mr. Andrews we kept you overnight for observation. I see you have been on anti-depressants. Who prescribed them?"

"It was Dr. Morgan, a psychiatrist," Logan replies.

"Oh, he's really quite good, though I've decided to book you for an appointment to see Dr. Amanda Smith, who is a respected psychiatrist in San Francisco. She's a specialist who has worked extensively with patients who have depression and mood disorders. So, I'm confident she can help you with long-term management of your condition."

"Well, thank you," Logan replies trying to appear encouraged.

"I have sent your file to her. Now I'm sure you are waiting for some good news: I'll discharge you. Before I do though, I have to ask you a few questions. Is that okay?"

"Yes."

"Thank you. Is it okay if I take notes and record our conversation?"

"I've no problem with that."

"Thank you," she replies, pushing the record button. "So, my first question: have you attempted suicide prior to this attempt?"

"No."

"Have you contemplated suicide before this attempt?"

"Only a few times when I was really down but I had no serious intentions to do anything."

"What precipitated this attempt?"

"I've just been feeling down... way down."

"Has anything changed in your life?"

"No."

"Any particular event or events make you feel down? Anything bothering or annoying you?"

"No," Logan replies, but it's a lie. He is especially annoyed with the stupid hospital gown they made him wear, which is even now coming undone but he is too tired to fix it this time. Then he adds because he really wants to get out of the hospital: "Doctor, seriously, I felt down before but I feel better now. With everything that's transpired, I no longer want to die."

"I'm glad to hear that. Now, do you have repeated thoughts about committing suicide?"

"No, just occasional thoughts when I feel down."

"Well, Mr. Andrews — can I call you Logan?"

"Yes, of course."

"Okay, Logan, how does life seem to you at present?"

Logan knows this is a trick question, so he considers how best to answer it. He doesn't want to reveal how he really feels. Then, he responds: "Well, life is a bowl of cherries. You never know what you're going to get."

"Hmm, I see, interesting, sarcasm." Dr. Knight scribbles and then she proceeds, "Do you ever wish you could go to sleep and just not wake up?"

"Well, I felt like that yesterday when I took the pills but I feel better now," adding with a smile, "thanks to the care that I've received at this hospital,"

Dr. Knight smiles and raises an eyebrow. "Thank you for the compliment, Logan. Now, I must ask you: Do you own a gun?"

"No."

"Do you feel anger at other people to the point where you would want to hurt them?"

Logan finds that's a strange question, so he replies with surprise: "No, never!"

"Do you think of harming yourself?"

"No, not now," Logan replies his voice showing some agitation with all the repeated questions. He wonders when the questioning will end.

"One final question, then we're done. Is that okay?"

"Yes."

"Have you made any specific plans to harm or kill yourself later on, some time from now? If so, what does your plan or plans involve?"

"I don't have any plan," Logan utters while silently considering different ways he would increase his odds of succeeding the next time.

"Thank you for answering my questions. Well, I lied. I do have one final question."

Oh, great, Logan thinks. *What does she want to ask now?*

"Do you have a ride?" Dr. Knight asks with a smile.

"No, I'll need to take a taxi."

"In that case, I will have one ready for you in 30 minutes outside our main entrance. The nurse will bring back your clothes and any personal belongings." She adds with a warm smile: "I wish you good luck."

Logan smiles appreciatively: "Thank you, doctor."

After Dr. Knight leaves the room and the nurse brings his clothes, Logan quickly dresses, glad to be out of the flimsy gown.

During the cab ride home, Logan looks out the window at birds playing across branches, and he reflects that precisely one year ago his life was destroyed and he'd never recovered. His life had become progressively worse and now it is the anniversary of his losses.

As night approaches, nothing seems right to Logan. The escape of work seems a distant mirage. He feels trapped. He was certain that even his co-workers noticed the low quality of his articles. Finally, Logan's mind reaches saturation and he is ready for sleep. He feels tired and exhausted, so he quickly falls asleep after switching off the lamp.

He goes rapidly from light sleep to deeper states. His eyes flicker and he enters into the secret world of dreams…

Holding hands - dancing in a circle as a grey bearded man in a navy blue turban and sky blue robe stands magnificently looking at the group. His sparkling grey-green eyes focus on Logan with an insightful and omniscient stare. A light surrounds his whole body like an orb filled with brilliant hues of a multi-coloured rainbow of red, white, yellow and blue. The colours glisten and flow into each other with an uncanny translucence that reminds Logan of some psychedelic vision. Yet, he hadn't taken any intoxicant to cause it, not even wine. What is it all about, he wonders? Concurrently with this thought, the man speaks with a deep, soothing voice. He greets Logan with the following words:

"Welcome! Welcome! This retreat has been created for you and others like you. This is where you will learn to connect to the Nexus. Trust your intuition - do not doubt the call that draws you here - and then you will be led spontaneously to our circle. Come! We are waiting." The voice trails off and the man disappears. There one moment, gone the next.

In the distance, Logan sees a mysterious, old stone house, which melts right into the landscape with huge maples and pines engulfing it, yet a magnetic force draws him toward it. Beside it is a tranquil stream with swans delicately gliding upon the surface.

****

Two days had passed since Logan was released from the hospital, the alarm clock rings for the third time after he hits the snooze button. He finally gets up with a start while staring blankly at the clock. *Oh God, it's 7:00 AM!*

He must leave in fifteen minutes with his article printed out. The shower, the toast with eggs and juice, and newspaper with the day's headlines are luxuries he cannot afford this Monday morning. He hurriedly dresses, and brushes his teeth and combs his hair. After printing out the overdue article, he rushes out the door.

Logan takes his briefcase out of the car's trunk but then he sees a rope there. He imagines: hanging by a beam—his body dangling, inert and lifeless. The thought of suicide frightens him but also strangely attracts him.

He shakes his head in disbelief as if to exorcise an inner demon. Last time, he didn't succeed because he hated pain but a rope though more violent would be more effective.

Finally he pulls the briefcase out and conceals the rope under some bags. He takes a deep breath when he's safely seated in his car. A turn of the ignition key and his two-year-old Honda Civic is ready to move. Logan heads out of the driveway and halts at the stop sign before heading for the interchange for the freeway.

Suddenly, Logan swerves his car, as he tries to miss a crossing cat. The cat is struck hard, and is tossed to the side of the road, where it lies motionless. As Logan anxiously gets out of the car, he hopes that the feline is still alive.

The cat's eyes are closed and the body is rigid; her back legs are crushed. The site revolts Logan, so he turns his eyes in the other direction. He walks away feeling dejected about his decision to move closer to nature because the harmony he sought is so elusive. Whatever he may want as a lifestyle, the drum of modernity beats on and simplicity becomes a muted voice able to merely whisper about a more uncomplicated life.

Logan wonders, why all this mad rush when beauty surrounds him? Still progress marches on, as it encroaches upon nature and her creatures, leaving no place for reflection and harmony. Even this road cuts through majestic trees, hills and valleys, interfering with nature's design. As a breeze moves trees, he feels his presence is unwelcome in this lovely landscape. Is it progress, Logan questions, when the earth, sky and water are polluted, and trees are cut down to make way for cars and cities?

He resolves he will not leave the cat's mangled corpse to be run over again. Instead, he will take it far away from the road. As he touches her side, he realises that she is pregnant. He had killed not only the cat but also the litter inside her. He takes a deep breath, feeling sick to his stomach.

After burying the cat under debris and earth, Logan takes out his water bottle. He washes away the blood and dirt from his hands. Suddenly he remembers his article and heads back on the road. He resolves this will be his last commute to work. One way or another, he determines to put an end to it.

Once he is on the highway, the rest of the journey to San

Francisco is uneventful; however he continues to be troubled by his strange thoughts. He feels that his heart is hollow and numb, without feelings.

Logan pulls into the newspaper's parking lot still feeling bewildered. To his delight, he has no trouble finding a spot because most employees haven't yet arrived. He surveys the three-story building that has been his work place for the past two years. Behind the glass windows, he knows there lies a monotonous sea of desks.

Logan trudges up to the bland building. He smiles and nods to Charlie, the fix-it man for the building, who is intently painting the wall and barely notices Logan as he enters the elevator.

Mary sits behind the receptionist desk on the third floor, greeting Logan with a warm smile. She adds cheerfully as he walks past her: "Good morning, Mr. Andrews!"

He smiles back and hurries into the newsroom. After opening the big glass doors with some effort, he notices the slow pace of the early morning and how much more comforting it feels instead of the noise of the workday. At one time, he found the racket exhilarating. Now, it just grates his ears.

The newsroom at first glance looks cluttered and disorganised. On further probing, you would realise the clutter has a purpose, particularly the desks whose surface cannot be seen under a mountain of paper, files and notes. The large number of desks, stretching throughout the space, conceals the fact that the newsroom is divided into special beats covered by different reporters.

At the entrance of the newsroom is the library, which contains archives and photos. Next to it is the beat desk that covers the local news. This is where Logan has been assigned for the past two years.

Just as he puts his briefcase on his desk, he hears a friendly voice from a few desks up.

"Hey Logan! You got the lead?" Peter asks with concern.

"Yeah, I sure do!"

"Well, you've taken your time with it. You know, we

weren't able to put the paper to bed until 11:30 because you couldn't be bothered to hand it in! I had to submit my article on fiscal mismanagement in your place, and we know how exciting that topic is for our readers. Your interview with the new Police Chief and his policy of zero tolerance would've been the perfect lead."

"I'm really sorry but as I explained..."

"Explained, what? You know, this isn't like you. What's with you, anyway? Are you feeling all right?"

"Yeah, never better," Logan replies, with a forced smile on his face. He wants to tell Peter how he has felt but decides against it because he doesn't know how to explain it. His own emotions are a mystery to him. Besides, he doesn't want to trouble his friend and let the word get around the newsroom. Peter is a great friend but he can't be relied on to keep a secret.

"Johnson isn't going to be happy," Peter remarks in a subdued tone. "He's been asking me questions about you lately: whether there's something wrong, or if you're feeling sick. I've covered for you but you have to start pulling your weight. You just can't allow deadlines to be missed!"

"You're right, Peter, but..." The sentence goes unfinished: Victor Johnson, senior editor, has just arrived.

"Logan, would you come into my office, I want to talk to you," Johnson interrupts in a curt voice.

Logan feels his heart beating faster and his shoulders and neck tense in anticipation of the battle to follow. He hates conflict and isn't looking forward to stepping into Johnson's office. He can already see Johnson peering out of the glass partition, waiting for him like a predator ready to pounce on its victim. After a deep breath, he timidly enters with the door closing firmly behind him.

Moments later, Logan emerges from Johnson's office, breathing a sigh of relief. The meeting went better than he had imagined. In fact, Johnson suggested a vacation, so that Logan could get himself together. The pressure might be too much for him, the editor said, and a vacation may allow him to find some rest for frayed nerves. Peter had already left for lunch and Logan decides to join him at the cafeteria.

"So, how did it go?" Peter asked, looking up from a bagel and coffee.

"Better than I thought. He suggested a vacation."

"A vacation!" Peter yells incredulously. "Maybe I should miss deadlines if you get time off for it," he then retorts with a smile as he dunks his bagel into his coffee.

"Well, it's not extra time off," Logan explains. "He's just asking me to take an early vacation."

"Hmm, that sounds reasonable," replies Peter taking a second dunk. He clears his throat, and tightens his lips with a serious look. "If you have any problem, buddy, I want you to know that I'm here to help." Then, he adds with a smile: "At the very least, I can listen and you know how good I am at giving advice."

They both share a laugh. Logan insists on picking up the tab and as he takes out a twenty-dollar bill, Peter sees a picture in Logan's wallet.

"You're still carrying a flame for her?" he asks pointing to the attractive blonde in the picture.

Logan remains silent as memories flood his mind about Sarah. He feels remorse over losing her because she should have been with him. At length, he answers with a subdued voice: "I've always loved her."

"I know you have," Peter says soothingly. "Is that what's troubling you? You haven't had some action? A married guy like me is too tired to have energy with work and the kids. But you must want a woman to keep you warm at night."

"It's not like that, Peter. But, I admit that I get lonely. At least, you have a wife and kids to share your life with. I go home to an empty house where I can talk to the walls..."

"Look, buddy," Peter interrupts impatiently, "you can't stay stuck in the past — in what could have been. You've got to move on and I know a gal who's crazy about you in this very office."

Logan raises an eyebrow. "Who?"

"Mary, the receptionist, has been eyeing you. You can tell when you look at her that she's interested. If you weren't so self-involved, you would notice that she is too shy to approach you, but she has tried to give you many opportunities to initiate something with her. Just go up to her and ask her out."

"Really?" Logan asks. "Mary's interested? Charlie also told me she's interested in me…"

"Charlie?"

"Yeah, Charlie, the fix-it guy."

"Oh, okay," Peter replied with a puzzled look on his face. "I'm not sure who you mean but he sounds wise, a lot like me."

"I'm surprised you haven't met him since he's always busy fixing something in the building; you probably just haven't run into him."

"That makes sense, I guess" Peter says with a yawn. "Now, getting back to Mary. Will you stop analysing it to death and just ask her out?"

"Well, okay," Logan hesitantly replies but he is preoccupied with the past - until he realises the conversation has to end because they need to return to work.

Back at the newsroom, Johnson has a new assignment about which he wants Peter to make calls in order to investigate if a good story line could be framed around it. A spiritual teacher, a guru of some sort, has been invited to speak at Berkeley on the connection between Quantum Physics and Mysticism. He is a retired university professor, who often speaks on spirituality even in his retirement. The information came over the wire, and Peter wants to establish a local connection between the man and his visit to the Bay area. He will make calls to create a profile before he tries to interview him.

Peter intently looks at the accompanying photo. The man's serenity and glowing face impress him. He takes the photo over to Logan, who is busy packing up items from his desk in preparation for his four-week sojourn.

"You lucky dog," Peter interjects with mock indignation. "Are you also packing the sun-tan lotion and Speedos?"

"Hey, Peter," Logan objects, "I haven't even decided where I'm going. I might just decide to take it easy and rest. It might be just what I need."

"Well, whatever you do, make sure you forget about this place. You deserve a break and when you come back… you can be your old self again."

"Yeah," Logan shrugs, "that's what I'm hoping."

"Oh, by the way, I've been given a new assignment about a visiting lecturer. I was struck by his peacefulness," Peter remarks while holding up the photo.

Logan stares at it intently. His face goes white as if horrified by an apparition. He is left speechless, looking fervently at the picture. After regaining his composure, he asks: "Who is he?"

Peter replies, "I had the same reaction. Doesn't he have an amazing serenity?"

"Yeah, but I've seen this man before in a dream. It's the same face, beard and turban."

Peter looks alarmed. "Hey, Logan! Take a hold of yourself. Have you been watching too many shows about the paranormal? Are you really even sure this man was in a dream you had?"

"Yes, I'm sure it's him. He was asking me to join him in some sort of retreat or something."

"Wow, that's amazing! It says here, he's leading a retreat in Ontario, Canada. Near a town called Elora. What a nice name for a town: EH-LOH-RAH. It has a nice ring to it, doesn't it?"

"Yeah, I guess so."

"Hey, I've got an idea. Why don't you go there, for your vacation? Visit Canada — see the beavers, the moose and find out if people really live in igloos..."

"They don't," Logan interrupts curtly. "I was born in Nova Scotia, Canada, lived there until I was fourteen and my parents moved us to the States. Canada's a great country – big cities and small towns, an outdoorsman's paradise..."

"Whoa, lighten up a bit. I was just kidding about the igloos crack – I know half of Hollywood is from Canada, and I'm sure Pam Anderson, Keanu Reeves, Rachel McAdams, Jim Carrey, William Shatner, Dan Akroyd, John Candy, Martin Short, Michael J. Fox, Eugene Levy, Tom Green and... the rest of them didn't come here wearing parkas. But it sounds like you really miss the place – an outdoorsman's paradise is it? Sounds like an ideal place for a vacation."

"Maybe so," Logan ponders.

"And, while you're there," Peter adds as he points to the picture, "try to figure out why you would dream about this guy? It could be fun."

"Well, I don't know," Logan says hesitantly. "I'll have to think about it but give me the information on the retreat."

"Sure, take this print-out of my assignment memo and this details sheet. I'll print another copy when I'm back at my desk."

Logan takes the memo and details from Peter. Then, glancing intently at his watch, Logan announces: "I'd better get going before rush hour. I'll see you in a month."

"Sure, buddy. Send me a postcard or something, wherever you decide to go," Peter affirms with a smile. He continues in a jovial tone: "Have fun and think about me working my butt off here!"

Logan waves good-bye to his friend with a big grin on his face yet his smile quickly fades outside the newsroom.

As he enters the elevator the mental fog returns with strong feelings of despair and trepidation.

The feeling of being stuck in work he no longer enjoys creeps up on him, making him anxious. He tries to maintain composure by mentally intoning: *Don't worry, Logan. You have a four-week break from this crazy place.*

Nevertheless, he knows a month is too short and concurrent with this realization; a piercing sense of loneliness and sorrow leaves him feeling uneasy as he remembers Sarah.

Images flood Logan's mind, as the elevator opens to the Lobby, of memorable but now painful times: walks by the beach, conversations shared with her about their dreams and hopes for the future, and the first time they made love on a beach with waves splashing around them.

His face contorts and his spinning mind seems like a trap. Thoughts of suicide and self-hatred come in full force. The same cycle of events that makes him feel that he is going over the edge repeats once again.

Panic fills his mind as he realises he will be alone for the next four weeks. He starts gasping for air, as his breathing becomes shallow and erratic. His heart starts palpitating uncontrollably. He knows this is it — he will die of a heart attack. Within minutes his whole body is drenched in sweat as the elevator opens to the Lobby, where he sits motionless, gripping his chest, on the bench.

His tight air passages slowly start to open and his breathing starts to return to normal. He is tired and unable to think, except for one thought: when will it end?

This time it does end when he is brought out of the experience as Charlie firmly touches his shoulder and stares directly into his eyes. He asks earnestly: "Are you okay, Logan?"

Logan nods his head, unable to speak a word. Finally, his faculties return but he feels exhausted.

"Charlie, could you help me to my car?" he feebly asks the building's custodian.

"Sure, mate, just lean on my shoulder," Charlie empathetically replies. Logan is glad that it was Charlie who found him in his condition. He wasn't one to ask questions; instead he would offer help without hesitation. Logan leans on him, as they make their way through the sliding doors.

The cool air outside clears Logan's head and by the time they reach his car, he feels good enough for the drive home. Charlie waves goodbye with a serious look on his face — a look that Logan does not see as the building and Charlie both become distant silhouettes in the greying twilight.

On the road home, Logan is overwhelmed by apprehension. He is alone again. The rope is still in the trunk where he left it two months ago. He always kept the rope nearby, as it gave him a grotesque satisfaction that he was the final arbitrator of his demise. His mind starts to wander, fantasizing about his death.

He wonders how people will feel once he is gone. Will they miss him?

Logan envisions his own funeral vividly: *The room is dim with his casket set on a table covered with many beautiful flowers. The light in the room somehow makes his black casket shimmer with an incandescent life.*

He hears a recognisable voice filling the parlour. The words are muffled but he is moved by the eulogy given by Sarah from behind the podium. She is shaken, hot tears streaming down her cheeks.

As the words echo in the silent room, his mother cries out loudly, asking: "Why, why!" She buries her head into her palms in disbelief of her son's suicide. Finally, she is calmed with a tight embrace by Logan's father. The whole room weeps and Logan feels a grim satisfaction while letting his fantasy swirl in his mind. Suddenly, the table swallows the casket, as it falls into a trap door and is immolated in a fiery blaze.

Logan is roused from his suicidal daydream by the sound of distant ambulance sirens.

His thoughts are disturbing because he realizes he is no longer in control. His precarious situation becomes even more evident to him.

Logan suddenly realizes that the time off may prove grave for him because he can't trust what he might do. An impending sense of doom sends cold shivers down his spine...

"A journey of a thousand miles
Begins with one step"
– Lao **Tzu**

2

Fated journey

Coffee, tea or milk? The question hangs in the air as the airline flight attendant looks intently at Logan.

Deeply engrossed in his thoughts, Logan fails to answer her. Finally, he replies: "No, I'm fine. Thank you."

After the brief interruption, he resumes his observations. The towering Rockies below at this height look like tiny models only a few inches high.

The plane increases its altitude and ascends into the clouds above. Logan sits alone in the window seat.

He lies back, and reflects on his journey. *Why did I make such a hasty decision to take this excursion? Did I make the right decision?*

Logan wonders what will lie ahead in Elora and mentally goes over trip details from arriving at Toronto's international airport to the ground transportation needed to get him to Elora and the site of the retreat.

He can hardly believe he acted so impulsively as to book a trip to a retreat based on nothing more than a whim and a dream of meeting up with the host of the retreat. Would this spiritual teacher truly be the man he saw in his vision?

Logan pulls the information Peter had given him from his pocket and again looks it over. The memo reads:

MEMO:
From the desk of Senior Editor Victor Johnson:

Peter, see what you can in the way of a story on this Chandra Singh guy. Maybe put together a profile and then interview him for the weekend Metro section.

He's a spiritual teacher, a guru of some sort, and he's been invited to speak at Berkeley on the connection between Quantum Physics and Mysticism.

The guy's a retired university professor, who often speaks on spirituality even in his retirement. He's holding a retreat up in Canada too – might be worth a mention, or a lot more if it's unusual or offbeat in any way.

Contact info and details on Berkeley and the Canadian retreat at Elora, Ontario are on next page and I left a photo of the guy at your desk. Have fun with this, do a little digging and see what you come up with. A lot of readers are really into this alternative stuff so could be a good, timely piece. As always, need this ASAP.
-     VJ

Logan next turns to the accompanying information sheet for some further details, including the specific location of the retreat, the costs involved and background information on the host.

After again reading through the material he refolds the pages again and returns them to his pocket. He closes his eyes, hoping to sleep and clear his mind. But it is not to be; painful memories of the distant past come back to haunt him…

Logan is now remembering the situation that had brought him out to California in the first place.

He recalls the day so vividly: the phone call from Dr. Cohen informing him that his mother didn't have long to live…

"What's wrong with her?" he had anxiously inquired, not wanting to hear the response.

"She is in the late stages of terminal cancer, which has spread into various areas of her body. Her condition has dramatically worsened and she has only a few months to live. I have suggested that she stay in the hospital's Cancer Ward, but she wants to return to her home. She needs palliative care and especially the care of loved ones. Does she have any family in Northern California?"

Logan remembers the anguish he felt over the thought of losing his mother — his only remaining connection to his early childhood. He had felt like a child again — wanting his mother to hold him in her comforting arms and say: "Everything is okay, dear. I'm with you, you have nothing to fear."

All the childhood monsters would vanish with her magical incantation. Now his mother was suffering and needed his help. He wondered what words he could utter to cure her, to take away the pain. He realized there were no words. He could only speak by his actions—by being there, by holding her and comforting her just as she did throughout his childhood. In that moment, he decided that he would leave his quiet cottage in Putney, Vermont, to make his mother's last moments as comfortable as possible.

His ambitions as a novelist had to be postponed. But, what about his other plans?

He took the engagement ring out of his pocket and intently gazed at it. He thought of still proposing to Sarah, even though he would have to leave for California. Why could Sarah not come with him? It would be so comforting to have her there by his side. Yet, wouldn't it be selfish of him to ask her to drop everything and go with him and endure his mother's agony? No, he couldn't subject her to that.

As he put the ring back in his pocket, Logan promised himself that when he returned, he would propose to Sarah on bended knee. Logan then surveyed the room, realizing that he didn't have much to pack. He saw a youthful photograph of his mother on an end table. She looked beautiful with her long, blonde hair tied back and her round, glowing face. Logan knew that it was not only his duty as a son to be there for her but his heart could have it no other way.

His mother's name, Nicole, is associated with victory. However, with the cancer having spread through her body, her indomitable spirit was crushed. She was a woman who did not run away from adversity but found courage within her to conquer all obstacles. If one frailty could be found in her, it was faithfulness; a trait she exhibited, even when the recipients of her affections were unworthy, like her father and husband. Both of them failed her and made her life difficult. They loved the bottle more than life itself, and had neglected their families in preference of their bar companions.

Her father worked hard on the family farm but drowned his money in booze. In the end, the family was left destitute when they lost the farm. At sixteen, Nicole had to find work in the city and she was thankful for the work she found cleaning houses. She met John, Logan's father, three years later, at a wedding for one of her friends. He was the groom's friend and had a reputation for partying. They quickly fell in love and in a year they married each other. John's fondness for drinking bothered her but she ignored it, as he only got drunk on rare occasions.

His merriment became progressively worse as alcohol mixed with gambling and formed a dangerous combination. By the time Logan was born, John had become a fulltime alcoholic. He was the kind of man who wasn't suited to family life, or more accurately family life did not suit him. He wanted adventure and freedom, and alcohol became his means of escape. At first, he was away for weeks, and then months until his partying reached a feverish pitch. On Logan's thirteenth birthday, he disappeared for the longest period. He was not seen for the next eight years, leaving Nicole alone to raise Logan during the child's adolescence.

Logan's father had resurfaced at a time when Nicole had re-established herself with hard work and diligence. Their son was an adult: independent and completing college, a degree in journalism. It was difficult for Logan as he didn't know how to adjust to this man who claimed to be his father, but had abandoned him during his teenage years.

No satisfactory explanation was offered and when pressed, his father would apologize and in the next breath add: "Well, shit happens." Logan could smell the stench of alcohol on his breath, though his father would initially deny drinking. Eventually, he would admit that he only had a sip to keep warm.

At the same time, he spared no expense at wooing Nicole to regain her trust. When she had fallen in love with him again, he asked her to move with him to Northern California. Logan thought that it was a terrible idea, but to his credit his father seemed to have sobered up, and had made a name for himself in sales for a wholesale company. Within a month of John's arrival, Nicole was eager about moving with him to California.

Logan had asked her in a perplexed tone just before she had left, "Are you doing the right thing moving with him? Can you trust him?"

She smiled sympathetically, replying: "Look, dear, I really don't know but I can tell you I am a one-man woman. Even after all these years, my affections are only with your father. Besides, he had a drinking problem back then. He's overcome it now. So he's a changed man. Don't worry. Things will work out this time. I have faith."

Logan did not reply but remained quiet until he realized that his own selfishness and fears might be standing in his mother's joy. He then replied: "Well, whatever makes you happy." He smiled, hiding his uneasiness.

It was just one year after the move to California that Nicole was diagnosed with last stages of cancer. Even with treatments of chemotherapy, it continued to spread.

John had started to drink again unable to deal with the stress. He did try at first but eventually he reverted to old habits.

Then, he disappeared again, abandoning Nicole at the most critical time when she was hospitalized with no hope of recovery. He had died in a car accident, drunk at the wheel, crashing head on into a transport truck. No one else was hurt but John died instantly from the impact.

Logan felt less sorrow over his father's death but more regret. Often, he wished to see the best in him but he couldn't forget his irresponsible behaviour.

And now... Logan had recalled the time when he was walking with his father from school. He was in Grade 5. His father said something that penetrated Logan's young mind: "Son, I hope you never grow up to be like me. I'm a disappointment."

In the next breath, his father took out a bottle of brandy and sipped it with a contorted face. He added: "Never get hooked on this poison. It'll ruin you!"

Logan knew even at that age that John never wanted a family and didn't really love him. Maybe, Logan reasoned, it was because he was an ordinary kid, not meriting his father's attention.

In John's own childhood, he had suffered some sort of abuse from his parents. It was something he never fully revealed. But he had confided in Nicole one time how he never had a real childhood. His parents would only speak to him in harsh tones and his father often spoke with fists. Logan could understand that his father must have also suffered; still he had fallen all too readily into the life of an alcoholic as an escape. He could have attempted to overcome his addiction and difficulties but he didn't even try. Sadly, life doesn't offer many chances.

Logan agonized whether or not to tell his mother about his father's death. After visiting her in the hospital, he decided it was best not to trouble her. She was too frail to take another blow. Instead, he suppressed his ambivalent feelings toward his father. Those suppressed feelings combined with the constant agony of watching his mother suffer, made his stomach burn and he would often get indigestion during those months. Eventually, he quietly accepted everything as some or sort of cosmic design or absurd game, he didn't understand.

He wouldn't have survived those days if it were not for the constant support of Sarah. She supported him unconditionally with boundless love and understanding ears. He felt release of emotional tension whenever he spoke with her. They were soul mates who understood each other in silence and in speech. He would often joke with her that if he came back as a woman, he would come back as her because they were so similar.

Their closeness extended into all dimensions from the joys of physical sensuality and playfulness, to the heights of exploring sublime realities in thoughts, words and life. They inspired each other with the intoxicating elixir of love's inspiration. No two lovers could be closer, or hearts more intertwined. They both firmly thought the cord that bound them could stretch far, but it would never break.

Logan recalls what he said to Sarah when explaining his mother's condition: "I received a call from my mother's doctor, Dr. Cohen. He tells me that my mother doesn't have long to live. She needs me. I don't want to leave you but I need to be there, with her in the final days and hours she has left..."

"I'm *so* sorry, Logan," Sarah had responded. "Your mother has fought hard and I can only guess the dreadful pain that she must be going through. How are you holding up?"

"I don't know. I really don't know."

"Sometimes feelings can be so overwhelming that you just feel confused by them," Sarah consoled. "We're together, Logan, so don't worry you can share everything with me. Okay?"

Logan took her head and placed it on his shoulder and kissed her forehead. He knew that he did feel tired and overwhelmed. The last few months were all too much with his writing career just ready to take off. Then, in the last three months his mother's health had deteriorated. He made numerous trips to San Francisco to be with her, and now with so little time left, he had decided to be with her until the very end.

Sarah took Logan's hand and looked warmly into his eyes. "Logan, go to California. Don't worry about me. Just know that I'm here for you and I will pray for you and your mother."

Logan considered himself extremely fortunate for having her love. Knowing that he could count on her made his responsibility less draining. She gave him the photograph that he continues to carry in his wallet to this day.

"Keep this photo with you," she had told him, "and when you see it, you will know that I am never too far. It's an affirmation of our ceaseless love that spans all distances. It's the picture you took of me in my red dress just outside the theatre. You took it when we went to Broadway. It was my first time in the Big Apple. Everything was so magical, since it was the holiday season with snow on the ground and Christmas lights everywhere. Best of all, I was with you. We spent the evening under the full moon and stars, walking hand in hand."

Logan had kissed her again.

Sarah had smiled and added, "That was fun, wasn't it?"

"It sure was," he had said with a smile but his expression soon became concerned again.

Sarah had again responded with comforting words: "If things seem too much, never hesitate to call me. I know that you can hide feelings; that you can be strong. I love you, no matter what. Don't try to be strong for me."

He nodded in reply and they hugged and kissed. In the evening, he had boarded the plane for California. Sarah had accompanied him to the airport, and waited until he had boarded the flight. She tried to be brave for him. But, she hated each time he left her alone. A tear rolled down her cheek with the thought of being without him, since she knew that each day would seem like eternity. She continued to watch him, as he became a distant figure dragging his suitcase beside him, until he boarded the plane and disappeared.

Nicole was a tenacious woman and she lived for another year. But, it was the most agonizing year for both her and her son. Logan's world became centered on her, but he was happy to be there for her.

The only regret was that Sarah had become distant from him. She no longer responded to his calls or letters. He wondered if she was angry with him for being away so long, or if she had lost interest.

If Sarah was angry, he would let her know that he didn't enjoy being away from her either. No one expected his mother to survive so long. Still, the poignant truth was that his mother's condition was terminal, and she had no chance of survival.

Then came the day mid-August when the expected happened. Around 12:45, Logan received the call from Ruby, the nurse who had diligently taken care of Nicole for the past year. She was tearful over the phone and her voice wavered. "Logan, come home quick! Your mother is dying!"

"I'll be right there," Logan replied wounded with grief. He had prepared for this day. Yet, can anyone ever really prepare to say good-bye for the final time?

As he rushed out of the office, Logan experienced such sadness that he felt he couldn't contain it. He felt like a child once again: Lost without his mother.

Even for a child who is an adult, losing your parent is like missing an essential part of the puzzle that forms your being. He didn't have closeness to his father, so when he died the hope of ever reconnecting with him faded forever.

With his mother, the loss was much worse, for she was the center of Logan's childhood. She was the connection to his inner child's triumphs and disappointments. Sometimes Logan like many boys had wanted to assert his independence by cutting the apron's strings. He didn't want to be teased for being a "mama's boy." Still, his mother was the one who was always there for him whenever he experienced any hurt or pain.

When Logan felt like a loser after failing Grade 4, his mother was there to lift up his spirits and give him confidence in his abilities, which is the greatest gift a parent can offer to their child. Other boys had their fathers to play with and guide them, but Logan always had his mother. He could always count on his mother... but no more...

As the taxi reached its destination of his mother's home on Market Street, Logan felt both anguish and a kind of release like the release felt after a stirring climax of a play when the emotions have been aroused repeatedly to such a degree that it feels almost like torment. If the play continued longer, all tears would dry up. Logan remained hushed, as he entered the house; an ominous silence filled the air.

Finally Ruby appeared. "I'm glad you're here, Logan," Ruby greeted him. "I know you'd want to be here at this time."

They walked into the bedroom where his mother lay. She was plugged to a respirator with tubes in her nose. Her lungs were congested with mucus and her breathing was raspy.

Logan sat beside her and held her hand. "Mom, can you hear me?" he whispered tenderly in her ear.

She didn't reply but weakly squeezed his hand in acknowledgment. When she tried to speak, only an incoherent gurgle could be heard. While her words were hard to make out at first, listening attentively Logan then understood them.

"...I love you son... go to Sarah... go to Sarah..." with these words she breathed her last. Her hand let go and her head tilted to the side. Her face, which had remained tortured with pain, lost its tension as the lines of pain vanished in an instant. The room remained silent as Nicole Andrews breathed her last breath, and ended her yearlong struggle.

Logan still feels the grief from that day as he sits reflecting on it during his flight. Now his mind turns to his return to Vermont after Nicole's funeral. He had felt drained but he looked forward to meeting with Sarah to reconnect with her and share his grief. It was a cold February day and the flight was almost cancelled due to the snow.

Even with the snow falling around him, Logan felt warm inside with the knowledge that he would soon see his Sarah. He could finally unburden, for Sarah would heal him with each kiss, each touch.

Logan arrived in Putney in a rented car battling the blowing snow and ice along the way.

As he pulled up to Sarah's house, he noticed the curtains were drawn but there was a dim light on upstairs.

He rang the doorbell, wondering what he would say to her first. He wanted to explain to her about the agony he went through and how he was lost without her.

The door suddenly opened and Sarah stood there surprised and puzzled. "Logan? What are you doing here?"

It was not the warm greeting that he expected. "Well," he replied, "I came to see you, Sarah."

A strong, male voice spoke from inside the home: "Who is it, honey? Is it someone for me?"

"No, Kurt, it's an old friend who was just passing through," she answered turning her back to Logan. She then looks at him with a serious, aggrieved look and declares with a solemn tone: "Logan a lot has changed over the past year and I couldn't wait any longer. I didn't know how you felt... I had to move on... I hope you understand."

She waited briefly for a response but hearing none, then tersely added: "I must go now." With those words, she shut the door on Logan. He continued to stand outside for a couple of minutes, completely perplexed and hurt.

As a gust of air made the snow swirl around him with a terrific howl, he resolved to leave. He wanted to walk away with a shred of dignity.

Logan's heart sank. All of his dreams of the warm meeting with Sarah were brutally dashed, for Sarah was no longer his. *What a cruel twist of fate*, he thought bitterly.

Logan had pulled the ring out of his pocket. His hurt turned into rage as he threw it away like a cursed object. It flew through the air, and fell on a rock, making a "ting" sound.

As he pulled out of the driveway, he had looked back at the house in misery. He realized he just wanted to get away from Putney and get back to San Francisco. He had decided to take the job as a reporter, and never come back to his hometown so long as Sarah was not his.

The work had kept him busy, so that he could suppress his sense of loneliness, sorrow and anguish. Unlike his father, he couldn't drown himself in booze. But work provided a good substitute, a welcome distraction from emotional pain.

Everything went reasonably well, or seemed to, and he continued to overlook his emotional state until despair set in with a vengeance. The feeling was overwhelming and took full control of him, battering his ability to fight, his will to live. He wanted nothing more than to end his misery by ending his life. He began contemplating suicide and decided to take this course of action. Finally, he ended up in the hospital from a failed suicide attempt after overdosing on sleeping pills.

*"Close your eyes and you will see clearly
Cease to listen and you will hear the Truth"*
-Taoist poem

3

Mystery and Enchantment

Sarah McMaster saunters leisurely beside the softly flowing stream in an Elora park, not far from the cabin she's booked for a vacation getaway.

Her spirited eyes glisten with the same sublime blue as the stream when kissed by the mid-day sun. Her honey blonde hair dances wistfully in the warm summer breeze, as she carries a book of inspirational poetry in her delicate hand. Her faded jeans and tattered tee-shirt epitomize her as does the book that graces her side. She has a casual yet bookish demeanour. Yet, she is striking with her blue eyes, blonde hair and soft features. She is slender with tiny freckles on her face that are hardly noticeable except in direct sunlight.

As Sarah wanders along beside the stream she thinks about her boyfriend Kurt. She is only twenty-five years old and he is in his late twenties, earning a significantly greater income than she could ever imagine. Even with the money, he is a troubled man and Sarah just wants a peaceful life.

Why is it such hard work to create harmony with him? she wonders uneasily.

Sarah glances at the profusion of day lilies growing in rich luxuriance beside the stream. Such vibrant colours: orange, yellow, and gold. Then she observes a caterpillar crawling along a leaf. Suddenly, the caterpillar falls off and lands on the grass. Feeling compassion for the tiny creature, she gently cradles it in her hand and places it cautiously on the leaf.

Sarah's thoughts turn to Logan Andrews as they always seem to when she thinks about the past. She can vividly see him almost as if he was really there, yet he is just a vision. She remembers him with hesitant feelings. It seems like yesterday, when they first met in Montpelier, Vermont.

Logan's midnight black hair and trimmed beard contrast his clear grey-blue eyes. She remembers when they first looked into one another's eyes; it was as if they saw into the very depths of a familiar soul. Sarah admired the way Logan achieved success as a journalist. She fondly remembers his erudition, creativity and idealism, which always found expression in his writing.

When we were together he always told me how wonderful I was! Was it just his extended time in California that finally tore us apart? Was my true happiness really with him? Sarah hesitatingly ponders what was and what might have been.

Sarah's recurring memories of Logan always stir up troubling feelings of ambivalence. *Oh well, the past is the past,* she concludes as her vision of Logan fades. I feel so stuck in life! *At least here in this peaceful countryside setting, this wonderful little town of Elora, I can have a much needed escape.*

She glances off into the distance and notices a charming old stone building that seems to beckon her. Beyond the building, the green of gently rolling hills creates a picturesque and pastoral scene. As she walks closer to the building a majestic willow tree in the backyard sways above the meandering stream. The willow reminds her that brittle branches break, while yielding branches dance with the changing winds. *This place is just fabulous, more beautiful than I ever imagined...*

Sarah sits down beneath the willow tree, her back resting against its trunk, and she rummages through her handbag for a well-worn copy of *Mystical Poetry* by Deborah Morrison. Sarah then leafs through the book where she's marked some of her favourite poems that have inspired her and given her spiritual solace and guidance. She reads the following 18 poetry selections:

ETERNAL PLAYMATE

Dissolved into ecstasies
Overwhelmed with Divine emotions
Teasing and playing
Self-forgetful
A spontaneous transcendence emerges

Our eyes sparkling
With inner joy
The essence of Love
Enfolds us

And so loveliness blossoms
Anew in Your presence

Within one another
The nectar of Love
Overflows

I am tempted
To taste it eternally
My only desire
Is to be ever in your embrace

TIMELESS

Life is brief
Time is fleeting
Arise
Awake
And realize the
Self

FLAME

The all-embracing grasp,
Our soulful love…
One…

Manifest power, circulating energy
Conjoint souls are we,
Entwined in Divine play of
Amorousness, I adore you…

Enamoured by the very memory
Of your touch, Longing for the fullness of you,
Quiescence enfolds
The spheres of my being, yet a teardrop falls
And yet I am set ablaze, I wait for you,
To be both one and the other
Renewal…

Light my heart
With your flame
Angel-star

Whisper softly, let my heart take wing
Play our love game again and again
Ecstasy…

MORE THAN A MOMENT'S RAPTURE

His charm
Would have depth, mystery
Inspiration for me
In the moments following
His voice

More than an instant of
Rapture
His essence
Obscure, numinous
As if a decree from the Divine

His presiding power, his spirit
At play with my soul
Was luminescence,
Lightning,
The thunder of Jupiter

His closeness
As the distance between us
Was set free
Enabled me to glimpse
The eternal that was hidden
Behind the surfaces of the temporal
The essence of enchantment,
More than a moment's rapture

When I suddenly realized
That the spirit of his voice
Whispered
To the soul of my heart,
The dialectic of the sacred
Was Revealing and hiding, mystical...
Therein was the truth

CREATIVE SPIRITUALITY

Creation
Verging on the Mystical
Existence loved for its own sake
...Being... Being... Being...
The glory of Existence
Creative spirituality happening
...Doing... Doing... Doing...
A certain Divinity exists in
Everything
In Everyone
In all that is
All that flows
From the Divine Source
Creative Energy
A light that shines
In the dark
A light that darkness
Cannot overpower...
The True Light
That Enlightens One and all
Active
Imaginative
Playful,
Ever Flowing
Unfolding, the Divine
Creation is as ongoing
As we are
In the innermost realms
Of the Soul
Full of Grace
Of Truth
Of creative spirituality,
And ecstatic with heaven
That is set ablaze within,
Becomes manifest as mystical experience, as creativity
That reveals magnificent treasures
Beyond our imaginings

HUMILITY

Non-assertion of egoism, humility
Is the way
That helps in knowing
Divine Will, look within
As the Soul ascends
Into higher spiritual planes
From possibility to possibility

Understand the mystery of Self
And the universe, and always
Follow your star...

Pure spirit reigns supreme,
Everlasting joy and peace,
Rise into Universal Mind

Meditate and discover
Priceless jewels of Divinity,
Enjoy the incessant Bliss
Of perpetual joy
And Supreme Happiness

"SELF" RELIANT

Abide in Eternity and Infinity
Oh Immortal Self, so True
Do not be dependant upon...
Abide in "Self" reliance
The highest of all virtues
Remember the Divine
Virtuous qualities
Of strength, power
As the key to peace
This is the essence
Of Spirituality

BLESSING

True Blessing
Is a pure heart
The key
That unlocks the door
Leading to the
Mansions
Of the Cosmos

Be patient
Practice Equanimity
Of Mind

Listen to the
Silence
And Be
In union with the
Divine
Love
With such intensity and
Be free
To proceed
With Grace

Give
Freely to all
According to the need
Of each

Follow spirit
With true dedication
Work as a humble servant
Unostentatious service, know that
All is received from the Divine
And all is humbly given to the Divine
Drink the Supreme nectar
Of transcending all divisions
Perceive the All within "One's Self" and
Peacefully abide

WHAT THEN MY LOVE?

Rare sensations
Awesome
Glimpses of the Eternal
Hidden
Behind the temporal

Our love
Like an ancient
Earthen pot of clay
Full of cracks

Like a house of old
Full of windows and
Doorways, incongruent and

Bent, not perfectly square

Our life together
Was full of cracks,
Nevertheless, my love,
Was that not where the
Unexpectedly numinous
Momentarily did appear?
What then, my love?

SACRED CIRCLE

Why does the snowflake melt?
To enliven spring flowers,
Why does summer sun blaze?
To ripen the garden,
Why does the leaf fall?
To bring forth beautiful snow...
Why do the seasons dance so?
To embrace us in the sacred circle

EVERYTHING FLOWS

The heart of imagination stirs
Deepening, ever deepening...
Soul seeks roots
Spirit desires wings
Tension arises,
Wherein the Divine sparks,
Connect
The Heavens unto the Earth
Shape, time and space
Enhance the heart...
And know that you can
Never step into
The same waters twice

COMPASSION

Suffering awakens desire for freedom and
Feelings of compassion for others
Through such life experience
Learn what suffering is
And come to understand
The sufferings of others,
Then life goes on...
With growing insight
And understanding
Capacity to feel compassion
For one another
Broadens, deepens
Rooted in understanding
Finally our hearts
Are warm with Love

PRACTISE LOVE

Never harm
Anyone
Non-injury
Is the highest virtue
Develop high thinking
Lead a happy, simple
Contented life
Be detached
Have forgiveness and be
Compassionate

EXPANSION OF THE HEART

True expansion of the heart
Is very, very rare and
The quick and ready
Impulse to give
Does not come easily to everyone
Large-hearted liberality
...Take everything and
Give to the other...
Then as real power
Blossoms into equanimity
A great dignity will radiate
Self-confidence
Quiet strength
Coupled with the force
Of a glance that is
Felt immediately,
Doubtless the direct outcome
Of a most merciful melting
Be content
Reduce your wants
And ever share
What you have with others

THE DIFFERENCE

There exists the difference
Between the mere "saying"
Of certain things and
Actually "Being" and "Doing" them
Oneself

People are not generally
Moved to action
By the words of a person
But almost unconsciously and
Inspirationally
By observing actual
Living precepts
Actually live
Exhortations uttered to
Evoke emulation,
This is the modern
Miracle...
The utter sincerity
Of one's life
Exacting correspondence
Of life actualized to

Beliefs upheld
Constantly endeavour
To embody in life
Whatever is spoken or written

DIVINE MELODY

Nearer to us than
Our hands and feet
Nearer to us than
Our own breath
Not to be found
In temples, mountain caves
Or forest fastnesses
Not hiding somewhere
Beyond the horizon,
Such joy on realizing
The Divine Melody
In our own heart,
Loving Grace of the One
That can connect our consciousness
With the Immanent Power
And take us to the place
Where the divine Melody descends

UNITY

Under seemingly great diversity
Flow unity and harmony
The essence of all is the same
The same Transcendental Reality
Underlies this world of appearances
All are waves of the same ocean

ENTRANCE TO THE GARDEN

Open French doors, framing the empty wicker chair
That overlooks the garden…

Threshold experience elucidated by use of
Space, symmetry, unity, movement and
Some prominent elements of form
A place or inner state of being
That is a liminal zone, neither here 'nor there

The entrance, a threshold space
Between being inside and being outside
Typically symbolic of a turning point
A change in consciousness
An experience where one appears to be still

Yet paradoxically there is great activity happening
On the inner level of one's being

And as a result one experiences
A transformation
From "here" to "there"
A literal transformation

Or perhaps on a metaphysical level…
Dusk, twilight, the moments between waking and sleep
Are liminal zones…

Threshold space and experience
Is why I am "seemingly" forever at the entrance to the garden…

****

Sarah puts the book away and stands and stretches, looking at the gently rustling beauty of the willow tree. *I am truly at the entrance to a garden in this wonderful space.*

"Admiring this peaceful paradise?" asks an unfamiliar voice.

Sarah turns around sharply and sees an interesting-looking couple standing emphatically behind her.

"Wonderful!" Sarah affirms, as she studies the pair carefully.

The woman with long, dark, auburn hair, hazel eyes and rosy cheeks, stands unassumingly youthful, joyous and radiant. She is completely relaxed in posture, yet energetic and elegantly dressed. Sarah takes an instant liking to her.

"Relax," the woman advises, while gently holding Sarah's shoulder, "and take in the beauty of nature, and enjoy your time here at our retreat." The woman's touch is pleasantly warm and Sarah feels a sense of relaxation throughout her body.

With a full, robust laugh the woman then asks: "Would you like a piece of chocolate?"

Sarah enthusiastically nods yes and graciously accepts a chocolate chunk from the large decadent piece in the woman's hand. The two have a fondness for chocolate and they savour its delicious flavour. The dark chocolate melts deliciously, with a bittersweet essence fit for the gods.

The woman looks up and smiles.

"My name is Celeste. I'm giving a lecture in the great hall of this quaint stone building this evening, with my partner Chandra," she explains, as she gestures toward the dignified man standing beside her. Sarah says that she would be most interested in hearing them speak, since the couple had aroused her curiosity.

Chandra is of East Indian heritage with a full, grey beard, deep, grey-green eyes and an olive complexion. He has a grandfatherly quality about him. Sarah feels comforted in their calm and peaceful presence.

"You're very welcome to attend – deeper understanding is the primary focus of our lecture. Deeper and deeper!" Chandra chuckles, with a resonating laugh.

Chandra invites Sarah to freely ask them for help with anything during her vacation in Elora and they would consider it a blessing to be of service. Sarah places her palms together in front of her chest and thanks them, knowing this to be a traditional greeting in India.

The couple smile, return her greeting and then take leave,

since they have to prepare the room for their talk. Sarah continues to watch them, as they walk together toward the entrance of the old stone building where the lecture will take place.

Sarah glances toward the willow tree in the back yard, and is now curious about the two people conversing under its branches.

She walks closer and sees a man and woman beneath the tree. The sixty-year-old woman is speaking to a rather tense man in his mid forties.

Now there's a curious pair. Sarah observes with a hint of self-doubt. As she intently looks at the man, she realises he looks familiar. Where did I see him, she wonders? Oh yes, his face was plastered in the business section of newspapers because he was involved in knowingly, fraudulently manipulating the value of stocks in a large company that he owned. He was deceptive to many people just for his own financial gain.

The man puffs on a Cuban cigar, and flashes a thick money clip overflowing with one hundred dollar bills. Sarah hears him stating that he dislikes impractical people who overspend, and that if he continues with his frugal lifestyle, he will undoubtedly become a multi-millionaire again. Sarah notices his most distinguishing feature, an extremely sharp nose.

Sarah carefully observes the elderly woman's response: "I remember when my late husband made only a modest income but money didn't matter because we were together, we were happily married for forty years through all the highs and lows, until he recently passed away."

The woman stops for a moment, realising that conversing while standing wasn't very pleasant. So, she kindly asks: "Would you like to sit down with me at the café? Perhaps we could enjoy a cup of tea."

Sarah finds herself walking towards the pair and she notices the woman's snow-white hair and wrinkled complexion give her an aged, sagacious appearance.

"Can I join you?" Sarah interrupts suddenly, surprising herself with her boldness.

"Of course, you're most welcome to join us for tea, dear. I'm Muriel and this is Steven," she replies in a polite, inviting tone.

Sarah feels at ease instantly, more so with Muriel than with

Steven, who continues puffing away on his Cuban cigar with its aromatic scent floating in waves around them. Sarah wonders why he doesn't offer to buy the tea, especially with that huge wad of one hundred dollar bills that he was flashing around earlier.

As the three vacationers stroll toward the outdoor café behind the stone building, it is Muriel who readily offers to buy tea for everyone.

Sarah finds her generosity as refreshing as Steven's self-absorption is disconcerting.

As Sarah observes the contrast between them with interest, she notices that Steven stands around six feet tall, towering above Muriel's slight five foot one inch height. She has wonderfully warm eyes, which are her most distinguishing feature, and in contrast Steven's eyes are constantly shifting and when they fix on an object, they exhibit a purposeful glare.

While they wait for tea under the shade of a maple tree, Steven looks serious and reverts to puffing on his cigar. Sarah explains that she is on a holiday just to have a long overdue escape.

"This is the perfect place to clear your mind," Muriel smiles. "I remember when Pierre, my late husband, would always vacation with me here. This is the first time I've returned without him. It brings back such fond memories to be here again. My only wish now is to die peacefully, then to be with my husband again. I really believe we'll meet again," Muriel confides, as she looks carefully at her audience's response.

Muriel's joyous nature hides her loneliness as a widow. Her eyes are warm and kind, yet they have a hint of sorrow, which makes her even more likeable.

Sarah listens attentively as Muriel talks about her many years lived in North Bay, Ontario with Pierre. Both Muriel and Pierre were of French Canadian, Catholic descent. Now a retired schoolteacher, she is comfortable maintaining the same modest lifestyle as always. Muriel talks about her love of gardening and then shows Sarah and Steven her most precious possession: a gold necklace with a heart locket, and inside is a picture of Pierre.

"And this is what I cherish most, my golden locket," Muriel reveals, as she becomes silent and gracefully sips her tea.

Steven abruptly cuts in: "Well, I'm from Toronto, and I'm decidedly Agnostic: When I'm not working at my lucrative business ventures or investing money for others, I'm either jogging or I'm at business seminars, or wining and dining the ladies at the local dance clubs. I just bought myself a new sports car. It's a gem!"

Steven pauses, as if waiting for applause. Finding only silence, he continues: "I've come here for a holiday, one of my many holidays this year. Life couldn't be better. My strategy is really paying off and it's compounding exponentially. Yes, life couldn't be better!"

Sarah is confused with Steven. He says life couldn't be better and yet his facial expression is serious and perplexed. She wonders if there's more going on with him than his arrogant exterior would reveal.

His clothes are noticeably dapper, but Steven seems to consider them cool. He continues to puff on his Cuban cigar between sips of his tea. His hair is silver and thinning, almost bald, his eyes a piercing blue. His many achievements are obviously results of his over-exuberant diligence. Sarah cannot help but notice that Steven comes across as stingy, tense and restless.

While she admires his ability to make a fortune, Sarah questions his ethics. She wonders: *What kind of happiness does he think he's experiencing? But then what kind of happiness am I experiencing in life?* She politely listens to Steven go on and on about his seemingly endless list of achievements.

Steven asserts that his life goal is to rebuild his wealth as soon as possible. Sarah gets offended when Steven argues that according to his calculations both Muriel and she are overspending and that is why they had such little money in comparison to him.

"Why don't we go inside and see if the seminar is beginning? Would you like to join me since I just know it'll be interesting?" Sarah interrupts, hoping to divert Steven from further criticism of their spending habits.

Once inside, Sarah notices that the historic stone building is absolutely abundant with charm, character and warmth. The building itself is interestingly "magnetic," over 110 years old, a century home converted from a store into a combination home/retreat centre by Celeste and Chandra. Many vacationing guests are attracted here to participate in lectures, yoga, tai chi, meditation workshops, and creative spirituality lectures. The centre is always busy with some sort of workshop, seminar or classes and in the spring and summer Celeste and Chandra lead a workshop to a few special individuals without any charge.

Sarah glances about the main room or great hall as it is often called. The walls are of stone even on the inside. The ceiling is high and vaulted with huge beams of natural pinewood. The windows are from the floor to the ceiling along the back wall and provide a magnificent view of the stream, willow tree and the entire backyard and beyond.

Beautiful paintings grace each wall. A huge, soft, sand-toned carpet covers the floor from wall to wall. The entire room is elegantly highlighted in varied shades of earthy décor. Many cushions are scattered throughout, with two rows of comfortable chairs placed along the walls for those who prefer them to the cushions. An over-sized fireplace crackles as dusk descends and the night begins to cool. Sarah is deeply warmed physically and right to the very essence of her soul. Everything is so thoughtfully, lovingly, creatively placed for enjoyment and comfort. At the far end of the room, opposite the fireplace, sit Celeste and Chandra. They are joyously seated side-by-side and everyone notices their peaceful presence.

Suddenly, there is a tapping on Sarah's shoulder. Startled, she turns quickly to see who it is. Sarah is speechless as she suddenly sees a very familiar face.

"Logan!" Sarah finally exclaims. "What are you doing here?"

"I'm just taking a break from work for a while" Logan sighs dejectedly.

Sarah can't help but notice that Logan looks tired. He has a pensive expression on his face as he slouches slightly while conversing with her. Logan reminds her of a flower deprived of water, about to wilt and fall over. He appears so much unlike the confident Logan she remembers.

Pensively, Sarah experiences the subtle scent of sandalwood incense that permeates the room. She runs her hand slowly along the hard, cool stonewall. She feels the softness of the plush carpet with her bare feet. *Barefoot on the beach,* Sarah mentally exclaims. A vivid memory surfaces in Sarah's mind as she gazes at Logan. She remembers being together running barefoot along the beach. A wave rolls in and splashes their once dry clothing. They laugh playfully, soaked almost up to their knees. The beach is deserted; they're alone. They kiss and impulsively throw off their clothes. Carried away with the moment they passionately make love for the first time...

Sarah is jolted back to the present when Logan again taps her shoulder. "It's about to begin" he advises, joining the others who are seated on the cushions. As Logan gets seated comfortably on a plump cushion, he glances over at Sarah in astonishment. He still feels amazed at finding her here. What an incredible coincidence for them to discover one another in a century-old stone home in Elora, Ontario, so far from their hometown of Putney, Vermont.

"Welcome! Welcome!" begins Chandra. He continues: "This retreat is created for you. This is where you will learn to connect to the answers that are already in your heart. Experience enchantment. Trust your intuition — do not doubt the call that brought you here. This is where you'll learn to connect to the Nexus."

Logan suddenly notices that Chandra wears a navy blue turban and a sky blue robe just like the man in his dream. *He is that man!*

Logan tries to listen to Celeste and Chandra speak of 'Connectedness' while he struggles to concentrate and the here and now and not on the dreams that continue to haunt him.

"Remember that our purpose together goes beyond the simple exchange of information. As you vacation in Elora, listen deeply within yourselves. Listen more than you ever have before. Go deeper. Listen to the silence of your soul. Just let go, and go even deeper."

"This is where you will discover what you want to know. You will spontaneously gravitate toward certain people or places at particular times. This is your intuition at play. Trust in your 'Self'-trust your intuition. Such spontaneous experiences are purposeful, as everything and everyone is interconnected, which will be the essence of the unfolding mystery of our time together. This interconnectedness is the centre of Nexus. You will learn to go beyond the ego, and then the true Self will be revealed to your conscious awareness. The Truth is closer than your own breath!" Chandra affirms with confidence.

Next, Celeste rings in a melodious voice: "Let us share a time of going into the silence. Concentrate on your breath... inhale... exhale... move with the dance of the soul and directly experience your true Self!"

Sarah and Logan both ponder the mystery of finding each other at this retreat as they drift deeper into the silence.

Although Logan tries to concentrate, he is overcome with a memory of the past. He remembers running his fingers along Sarah's silken hair.

His mind returns to a time when they were enjoying a candlelit dinner that Sarah had lovingly prepared. She brushed her lips against his. Their delicious kiss was wild with passion. His longing hands gently, lovingly grasped her breasts. They rested upon the thick-carpeted floor and ecstatically fulfilled one another's desires...

"When any experience of body, heart, or mind keeps repeating in consciousness, it is a signal that this visitor is asking for a deeper and fuller attention."

\- Jack Kornfield, *A Path with Heart*

4

Where is Peace?

Days quickly pass by. Logan reflects on his ongoing retreat experience. He questions: *Why did I travel to Elora? What compelled me to come here with such little hesitation? How is it possible that I would meet Sarah here, so far from home? Were we meant to find each other again? How does she feel about me now?*

As Logan looks off into the distance, he observes two swans swimming harmoniously together in the tranquil crystal clear stream. As he sees the image, he remembers his dream that led him to this retreat where two swans also glided over the waters of a stream.

The correspondence between each image in his dream and his experiences at the retreat are so uncanny that Logan struggles between acceptance of this connection and its denial because its significance is disturbing to him: If he becomes consciously aware that he was somehow led to this retreat through his dream, then he needs to accept the mysterious in his life. His journalistic training to be objective and his desire to maintain rationality won't allow for something so threatening to his understanding. So he contemplates finding a way of losing conscious awareness and thus remain in ignorance and denial. Yet, the connections to his dream are all around him and they are hard to deny: Chandra was the grey-breaded man in the navy turban; even the old stone house, the stream, and the swans are all connected with the dream. Yet, Logan wants to deny this troubling association.

Logan thinks: *Now what did Chandra say to me in the dream. Oh yes, 'trust your intuition.' How on earth do I trust something I don't even know? You can't touch it or measure it, so how am I to trust it? For all these reasons, intuition seems such an unbelievable idea. You can't point to it and say I have found my intuition and how do you seek guidance from it?*

So, Chandra's words to Logan are like those in a fairy-tale: nice to hear but impractical and besides his intuition, if it exists, has a dismal record. It misled him to seek love from Sarah when she would only betray him. *So much for trusting your intuition.* With these thoughts, Logan is certain that his situation is hopeless.

Logan realizes that even in the middle of a paradise like this retreat, he feels hopeless.

His thoughts are broken as one of the lovely swans glides toward him and then unfurls its downy, white wings. With a flap of the wings he is skimming over the water and takes flight and soars above the trees with grace. How Logan wishes he could also take flight but he is earth-bound, unable to release himself from his physical bonds.

As the water is stirred once again, Logan notices the female partner nibbling on some hedges she has uprooted. At first, he doesn't notice the five young cygnets that gather around her to peck at bugs as their mother stirs the water.

They seem so tranquil, working with the pond's ecosystem for sustenance. In comparison to them, Logan knows he is cast adrift from his spiritual centre. To seek guidance would make sense but where should he turn?

His life isn't as simple as the swan family's existence within the natural world. Logan ponders: *Here I am on vacation, I don't even have the pressure of going to work, yet I still feel terrible. If I can't feel joy here, then I'm getting worse not better.*

Logan withdraws from the pond, unable to share in its beauty. The setting only magnifies his despondency. Logan returns to his cabin, so that no one, not even the swans, can see his loneliness. His intuition is telling him that it's hopeless — really hopeless.

The only escape from this hopeless existence is to end it or at least to be intoxicated into oblivion, Logan concludes. *Seeing Sarah has only opened old wounds. Things are getting worse for me, not better. I need to somehow escape.*

Logan lies back on the bed in his cabin. Images surface about how he will either end his life, or at least lose conscious awareness through sleeping pills, starving, or perhaps alcohol. Well, why not follow his father's example: *The apple doesn't fall far from the tree. I'll drown my sorrows just like my father did. I'll get it over with tonight.* Logan elaborately plans the evening in his mind.

Then Logan suddenly jumps two feet into the air, as he hears someone calling out his name:

"Logan! Logan!" Steven calls.

Logan drops to the ground with a heavy thud. "What is it?" he asks, as he rubs his sore foot and tries to appear relaxed.

"You know," Steven says excitedly, "I think I've figured out how you can experience greater joy in your life!"

"How" asks Logan? Then he adds: "I'm happy enough."

"It's really so simple," Steven explains, "I just can't understand why more people don't think of it. You decrease your expenses and don't give to anyone but yourself, and then through investing money in a diverse portfolio the money increases, exponentially. That's what I've done and it really works."

After a brief pause waiting for a reaction that doesn't come, Steven continues: "Even though I've had a six-figure income, my expenses have always been kept at a minimum. I buy my clothes and furniture from a second hand store and live in a small apartment. The only luxury I have is my new sports car, but that is just to impress the ladies," advises Steven.

"Well I'll just keep that in mind," Logan strains trying to appear thankful for the advice.

Later that evening back in the old stone house: The circle of Logan's dream is formed and everyone holds hands, as dusk falls and the day quietly transforms into evening. Chandra in his navy blue turban and sky-blue robe stands magnificently looking at the guests. His sparkling grey-green eyes focus on Logan with an insightful and omniscient stare.

A light surrounds Chandra's whole body, like an orb filled with brilliant hues of a multi-coloured rainbow of red, white, yellow, blue and violet. The colours glisten and seem to flow into each other with an uncanny translucence that reminds Logan of some psychedelic vision. But, he hadn't taken any intoxicant to cause it, not even wine.

Yet, Logan intends to get drunk this evening and to lose total consciousness. *I'll save the alcohol for later this evening,* Logan promises himself.

While in his deluded fog, Logan comprehends that his dream that guided him to this retreat was a premonition. The dream's images are becoming present reality, as the aura (the brilliant orbs), around Chandra's body expands. Amazingly Logan is able to see the aura. He can't believe his eyes, yet the mysterious is right before his eyes. He wonders if anyone else can see the brilliant colours surrounding Chandra's body.

As Logan perceives the aura, he mentally hears Chandra's voice communicating with him: *Logan, what you're witnessing is the energy field that surrounds all life forms. It's the Chi spoken of in China and Prana spoken of in India. This energy connects all beings. Ordinarily we cannot apprehend it but know that it is always there, connecting all beings to a greater, universal energy and flow.*

As Logan looks around, he can glimpse the same aura surrounding each guest at the retreat. When he looks at his own hands, he can also perceive it. Even the very landscape of rivers, animals and rocks seems permeated by it. Truly everything does seem connected by this flow. However, as a dark thought-cloud shadows his mind, the whole scene changes to a grey, shadowy landscape of twilight.

Yet, Celeste stands out in the bleakness with a near angelic light surrounding her, so Logan's attention now focuses on her. She is both emotional and penetrating.

Dressed in deep forest greens her skirt flows freely about her ankles. She is of Irish descent, having an affinity for Celtic lore and story telling, with eclectic spiritual tastes.

Celeste has resided for many years on Salt Spring Island, one of the Gulf Islands on the Canadian West Coast. She retired from a successful career as a classical violinist and found her partner, Chandra, late in life, to share their remaining years together at their home in British Columbia. Her laughter is full, robust as she affirms: "Listen carefully to your True Self. Remember, in a world where you often put on masks and take on roles, you can stay connected with who you are. The first step is to listen with awareness, especially for things that you don't yet understand. The understanding will develop in time and through grace. Critical examination is highly important, yet reason and intuition need a balance between them."

Logan considers Celeste's words and feels a connection with her. He has noticed that she is the one who always makes sure that the candles are lit, the incense is burning and fresh flowers are placed artistically around the room. If only he weren't so troubled by Sarah, Logan would allow himself to be receptive to a fuller experience at this retreat.

Now, Logan shifts his gaze to Sarah. She looks so beautiful in that moment, especially because her shyness is lost in the circle dancing. He wonders what her true inner feelings are for him. Whatever they are, he believes he can't have her, so Logan suppresses his desire and love for her.

Logan really wants to escape. The retreat is meant to be beautiful and inspiring but Sarah's presence is too much for him to handle. He confirms his plans to go into town and just get completely drunk. At that moment, he starts to feel forgiveness for his father. Logan realizes how difficult it is to change, to let go, and to listen to new awareness. He faces a struggle between desire for new awareness and a desire to remain in denial, especially to thoughts that necessitate major paradigm shifts.

He is brought out of his thoughts when he looks at Steven's crazy disco moves. It's hilarious! Still, he admires Steven's sense of daring to try, even if he looks completely foolish. He wonders if beneath his haughty exterior, lies a great story. As a reporter, he knows that often to get at the truth; you have to dig beneath the surface. But, he doesn't even know the workings of his own inner world. Why does he feel so awful? When people at this retreat are around him, why does he feel so lonely and disconnected? Maybe, he just needs to stop thinking because the labyrinth of negative thoughts leads nowhere.

Logan hears Muriel's open laughter. Yet, he knows she also suffers loneliness, all alone toward the waning years of her life. Her favourite possession, the gold necklace glistens in the candle-light. Logan concludes that even a happy life ends in sorrow, suffering and loneliness.

Giving in to the joyful atmosphere, Logan decides to join the others who have already begun an opening dance. Together they sway in a circle and finally flow spontaneously into ecstatic dance. He begins to feel somewhat better inside from the movement, as if energy blockages are released. He imagines for a moment the energy flowing with greater strength into every cell of his being.

With the positive reinforcement from the dancing, Logan decides to participate in the yoga class.

Chandra begins with a guided meditation on forgiveness: "Forgiveness allows freedom from the sorrows of the past and it allows for reconnection at a personal and interpersonal level. Also forgiveness is a way to soften the heart and release our inner obstacles to experiencing total peace. It is one of our greatest gifts for oneself and for others. Ultimately, forgiveness requires awareness of the hurt and pain behind the anger we feel. If we deny these feelings, then we cannot really forgive either ourselves or another person."

Logan considers the importance and meaning of the meditation as Chandra pauses briefly and then continues: "Keep in mind that forgiveness does not mean that you have to associate with someone who has caused you harm. Perhaps you will never see them again. Forgiveness is from the heart, a letting go of resentment and pain. Before arriving at forgiveness we go through many phases from denial, to hurt, to anger and then to acceptance. It is an integrated adjusting of one's life and entire being. Thus the process of forgiveness goes from experiencing the hurt to finally letting go and no longer carrying the pain."

Another brief pause, and Chandra adds: "Visualize others that you may have knowingly or unknowingly hurt... Now silently ask for their forgiveness. Then envision your own body. Let yourself see any hurt that you may have caused yourself. Notice if you hold lingering hurt in any part of your body as tightness or rigidity. Then ask for forgiveness for yourself and release that energy."

Chandra took several deep and relaxing breaths. "Now visualize anyone who may have hurt you or caused you suffering. Feel the sorrow. Feel it fully: see how it weighs on your heart, how it may constrict your lungs and excite your thoughts and passions. Now, to the extent that you are ready, offer your forgiveness to them and thereby release the pain that you have carried in your heart for too long. Let go of the past and open your heart to each new day with compassion."

Chandra brings the meditation to a close as he says: "Gently bring your awareness back to your breath. Focus on each inhalation and exhalation. Gradually bring your awareness back to your body. As you slowly open your eyes maintain an awareness of inner peace."

Next, Chandra begins to demonstrate some yoga exercises: "First I will show the headstand," he says, as he folds his hands and begins to assume an inverted posture. Chandra holds the entire class in awe as he does the headstand with poise and perfection, resting his whole body on the tripod of his head and arms. When he comes down, he winks and smiles: "Not bad for an old guy."

"He makes it appear effortless," explains Celeste, "but, take your time, practice with patience until you can do it with steadiness. Remember not to rush and if you can't do it yet just practice the shoulder stand. Let me demonstrate it." She lies on her back and with her hands she supports her back as she slowly elevates it.

Then, Chandra adds: "For those of you who feel comfortable trying the headstand: There are five basic steps to correctly enter into the headstand posture. What is most important is not to put too much weight on the head, but rather balance with your arms.

Also, remember to only lift the legs straight up once you've secured your balance. Finally, be aware of when you have acquired balance, and only then proceed to lift the legs. Now anyone who feels comfortable give the headstand a try and I'll walk around the class to assist anyone who needs it."

Steven, being achievement-oriented and competitive wants to be the first one to do the headstand.

However, Steven's competitiveness has consequences that he soon discovers. "Ouch, oh help! I'm in pain! Ouch!" moans Steven as he crashes to the floor, "My back, my back!"

Logan feels bad for Steven, but he can't help thinking that if he had been more patient, he would avoid hurting himself.

"I'm okay," Steven assures. "I don't know what happened. Somehow I lost my balance."

Chandra inquires, "Did you have balance before you raised your legs?"

"I don't think so. Besides, the best approach to physical exercise is to just do it and not to worry about little things like balance."

"That approach works in many areas of life, my friend," Chandra smiles, "but not in the inner arts like Yoga, where you have to be tuned to your body, breath and mind. Yoga means union: of both body and mind. Awareness is very important in practice like yoga. To be aware you have to practice receptivity, which is the opposite of force. You engage in activity after listening. Am I ready to carry out this activity, or do I need to be patient until I know I can do it with balance? Listening necessitates silence, awareness and guidance rather than rushing into an activity. Does that make sense?"

Steven nods his assent and remains quiet, feeling bad about looking foolish in front of everyone. As soon as his back isn't sore, he's determined to show them all what a real headstand looks like. Then, he looks over at Logan, who hasn't even attempted anything.

"Well, Logan, aren't you going to try."

"No, I don't feel like trying anything."

"Why not?"

"Just don't."

Chandra interrupts them: "Logan, don't let Steven's experience dissuade you. You have to make mistakes in order to learn from them."

"I know but I feel no motivation for attempting it."

"I see. Do you want me to think of ways that you can reclaim your motivation?"

"If you want to but I really don't care."

Steven retorts: "Oh, you're just saying that because you're afraid that you'll fail."

"Maybe."

"Do you enjoy this melancholic act?" Steven asks.

"I wish it were an act," Logan replies.

As Steven makes a movement to put his hand on Logan's shoulder, he feels excruciating pain in his back and yells: "Ohhhh, my back!"

"Just lie still," suggests Chandra as he kneels down at Steven's side.

"I think I've aggravated a previous lower back injury. I'm in too much pain to walk. I can move my legs though, very slowly," Steven remarks as he wiggles his toes.

Chandra moves in for a closer look.

"I know what's happened – it's that disc in my lower spine" groans Steven. "I had a pinched nerve there before and the pain normally goes down my butt and legs. Right now, oddly enough I feel it in my upper back and shoulders."

Chandra instructs Steven not to move and requests Sarah get a blanket to put under his neck. He gets his cell phone and begins to dial. "I'll have you checked out by Dr. Wellspring, she's the best doctor in town and she makes house calls," explains Chandra as he begins dialling. After talking to the doctor's office, he recommends: "Just take it easy, Steven. The Doctor will be here soon."

Chandra remains at Steven's side, as Celeste gathers the rest of the group toward the front of the room. She feels worried about Steven, yet she wants the evening to still conclude on a positive note. This type of injury has happened occasionally before, so she trusts Chandra to handle it. She wants the group not to lose focus; consequently Celeste begins a final relaxation exercise to complete the yoga class. She asks everyone to grab a mat, lie down and get comfortable.

Then she assures the group and begins the visualization: "Don't worry Steven is in good hands. I want you to relax... Let your breath find its own natural rhythm, easy and free flowing...just as life can be...effortless effort, action that is free flowing...begin to relax and let go" Celeste calmly guides the group into a deeper relaxation experience with her soothing voice.

When they reach a deep level of relaxation, she continues with a guided visualization: "Now, imagine or visualize a force-field like blue, glowing light all around your body. Wherever your body is relaxed this blue light permeates each muscle, each tissue, and each cell in that area, making all tensions vanish."

After a moment, Celeste continues. "Now, in some areas of your body you have tension caused by withheld emotions either of hurt or anger. Imagine these areas of tension as dark red vortexes that act as drains on your energy field. I want you to imagine that blue light is slowly reaching them... reaching them... now, permeating them... permeating them fully... and as it does, you feel release... Release from anger, hurt or pain."

Another pause, and Celeste adds: "Now think of forgiveness... forgiveness of someone who has hurt you and forgiveness of yourself for being angry. Now, take a deeeeeeeep breath... hold it... hold it for three counts: One - two - three. Now, breathe out all tensions. Breathe it all away and feel the release. When you're ready, come over to the cushions on the floor and we'll share in a talk."

As everyone finishes the guided relaxation and slowly gets up, they sit on the floor with comfy cushions to attentively listen to Celeste.

Time passes quickly and the yoga class is finished. Then Logan and Sarah walk together, unhurried, to the large window at the back of the room. They enjoy the view, the majestic willow tree that dances playfully in the breeze. Together they gaze at the wondrous reflections of the silver moonlight.

Sarah boldly remarks: "Somehow it seems so natural to be together this evening." She sighs as she looks right into Logan's eyes.

Logan maintains his pensive expression, as he struggles with his passionate feelings for Sarah and remains silent. He wonders why Sarah is toying with him.

To keep his mind away from lustful thoughts, Logan begins to think about Celeste's discourse on Yoga philosophy from the previous night:

Logan can mentally hear Celeste's voice: "To understand desires and then to channel them in the right direction is the only true way to happiness. In societies that emphasize instant gratification, the mind becomes dominated by constant desires and excitements. Mental purity and mental agitation cannot co-exist, so to calm the mind and attain clarity the mind has to be emptied of unrestrained desires, rambling thoughts and oscillating emotions. Meditation allows us to contact the mind's purity underneath myriad fluctuating thoughts and emotions. So, listening to your thoughts and emotions with awareness is an important first step in your meditation practice."

And Logan remembers another passage from Celeste's yoga discourse: "Also, remember that everyone's true nature is spiritual. Deep within is the ever-present inner centre of peace, which is the Nexus within. Misery and suffering emerge from ego and desire. Peace emerges as the ego is transcended. Once the ego is transcended then the Nexus is realized, in order to gain real freedom and happiness. To discover happiness look deep within, and experience your inner centre of peace during moments of silence and awareness. Know that this peace can be experienced in any and all conditions and circumstances in one's life."

Logan reflects carefully on these words, as he sits quietly beside Sarah.

After a long pause, Sarah breaks the silence.

"I experienced a deep sense of peace in the relaxation this evening – how was it for you?" Sarah inquires.

"Well, it was good. But, I feel other things besides peace."

"What did you feel?"

"Many emotions but I don't think you'd want to hear about them."

"Yes, I would."

"I felt hurt, really hurt. Now, why in the world would I feel hurt, Sarah?"

Sarah just smiles and remains silent.

He wonders: *How can she be so cruel to not acknowledge the hurt she caused me and instead to just smile at my misery?*

Logan holds Sarah's chin and gently lifts her face. He looks searchingly into her eyes, and wants to tell her he still loves her, but decides to maintain silence. Logan does not want to reveal his heart to her, in case she would break it again. He has no idea how she feels.

Yet as he looks attentively at her lovely face, he feels overwhelming attraction and passion for her.

He decides to reconsider getting intoxicated tonight. Perhaps his hasty drinking binge is not the only option. He admits to himself that really he wishes things were the way they used to be when he was together with Sarah.

Logan now realizes he experiences comfort just by being near her. He feels that it is only natural that they find themselves together on this evening beneath the full moon.

"Sarah, you look so beautiful this evening" Logan says in a warm voice "I really feel better when I'm talking with you."

"Well, thank you," Sarah replies. "We've known each other since high school. I've always enjoyed being able to talk with you. And, I'm glad I'm with you tonight."

Logan is encouraged by Sarah's reply. He was searching for any hint that would show she still wants him.

Logan loses all concern and leans forward to kiss her fully on the lips as he had in the past, but Sarah abruptly pushes him away. Her eyes look terribly cold and distant to Logan.

As his disappointment turns to seething rage, Logan smashes his fist through a large window. The glass shatters into a million pieces, crashing on Sarah and Logan, and falling in shattered pieces all over the carpet.

Logan is upset by his irrational action. He holds his bleeding hand and is in disbelief of his sudden outburst.

Steven limps toward them with a cane given to him by the doctor. He comments: "First I break my back doing a headstand. Now, Logan smashes his hand on glass. This retreat is turning pretty violent. If we could redirect our energies to business, we would make millions. What do you think, Logan?"

"I'm so sorry. I don't know what came over me. Sarah, are you okay? This isn't like me."

Celeste inquires about what happened: "What is the problem? How did this happen?"

Logan sheepishly replies: "I don't know how this happened."

"Don't worry about the window," Celeste says reassuringly, "let me make sure your hand is okay, and then I'll get some bandages for you."

While Celeste inspects his hand and carefully removes any glass with tweezers, Logan inquires: "Where can I find peace? I've certainly proven that it isn't in me. There isn't any peace anywhere. How can I fly with the eagles when I have broken wings?"

Steven retorts: "And, how can I fly with the eagles when I'm surrounded by turkeys?"

Change and continuity are two sides of the same coin
- Unknown

5

Wisdom of the Heart

Logan sits beneath the willow tree gazing at the sunrise and is unimpressed. *I'm so fed up with myself. I didn't even have the energy to follow through on my plan last night. Hopeless, it's completely hopeless. What does everyone see in that sunrise anyway? Every day they just wake up to the same problems they had the day before. Or if they're lucky they'll get new problems just for variety. They pretend to be enjoying the sunrises, when really deep down they feel just like me...disappointed and fed up. They're all wearing masks. At least I'm being real...*

He continues complaining in his thoughts, surprised and disappointed as well that everything has remained the same in his life, including his strained relationship with Sarah. And for this he'd given up his plans to binge on alcohol? *Maybe everything's beyond fixing, totally hopeless and I should go out and get drunk and forget all this...*

Suddenly his thoughts are disrupted by the appearance of a friend bringing tea.

"Logan, let's walk together to the old stone house," Muriel suggests. "The discussion for today is beginning soon," she adds as she gives him a cup of ginseng tea. "Here, drink this herbal tea on the way. I'm sure that it'll revive your energy and help those hands of yours to heal," Muriel smiles, as Logan grasps the cup with his bandaged hands.

"Be thankful that you've only got minor injuries," Muriel adds. "You could have easily seriously cut your hands or fingers when the glass shattered all over you. Glass like that shattering everywhere can easily blind or hurt someone badly. Yet, I know you didn't mean any harm by your actions. I'm just glad that you're not seriously hurt."

They both remain quiet.

Logan sips his tea and reflects on his previous night's outburst. He still can't fathom the source of his emotional rage and outburst. He feels even more troubled, wondering if he is a threat not only to himself but also to others. Is he really out of control, or is there another explanation for his sudden outburst of rage?

Muriel again provides a soothing, affirming voice: "Don't worry about it, Logan. We all sometimes act irrationally but we can always learn from our experience. You're a good person who seems to be troubled inside. Often when a person gets angry or acts violently its root cause can be hidden hurt or fear. I've never felt uneasy with you. So, don't be hard on your self. You can't change the past but the future can be built on wisdom gained from past experience."

As Logan hears Muriel's words he develops a fondness for her. He can sense that she genuinely cares for people.

"I think it's a miracle that you're doing so well." Then Muriel continues: "Isn't that the most beautiful sunrise you have ever seen?"

"Is it really that inspiring? The sun rises every single day, doesn't it?" Logan remarks. He looks gloomy as he fumbles with the cup held loosely in his bandaged hands, attempting to avoid an embarrassing spill.

"Are your hands bothering you? Is that why you're pessimistic?" Muriel inquires with a concerned expression.

"I guess," Logan shrugs, not really wanting to carry the discussion any further because he feels uncomfortable.

Logan and Muriel walk together to the old stone house where everyone is already beginning to sit down for the morning discussion. Logan and Muriel notice Steven limping along awkwardly with his cane as he struggles to slowly walk into the building.

He stops at the doorway and sharply turns toward Logan. Steven laughs loudly, as he looks at Logan's bandaged hands. He sarcastically comments: "Well, well, well. I suppose you've learned your lesson."

"You're one to talk after your display of back-breaking yoga" Logan replies defensively, finishing the last sip of his herbal tea.

"Well mine was just an accident, what's your problem?" Steven retorts and then turns to enter into the building, oblivious as to whether Logan had a reply or not.

"Never mind him Logan, he's just plain grumpy; don't take it personally," Muriel assures. "Let's just find a nice place to sit down, since I'm sure the discussion will be interesting."

"I suppose they're giving up on yoga classes for a while. We're pretty hopeless" Logan mutters. But Muriel doesn't hear him as the discussion was already underway...

The entire group is sitting in a circle on the floor. Chandra asks everyone to write on a blank paper about their reflections on the retreat, especially what they have learned or would like to learn if possible.

Steven walks up to Chandra and remarks: "I have nothing to write about with the retreat. Give me another topic."

"Okay," Chandra calmly replies. As he scribbles something on paper, he adds: "Try this topic then."

When Stephen sits down in front of the blank paper before him, he opens Chandra's folded question, "Tell me of a time in your life when you experienced true love in your life. What was your experience of it? How did it make you feel?"

The question takes Steven off guard. He remembers how after years of feeling lonely, he met a special woman, Diane, while vacationing in Northern Ontario. His obsession for money became secondary when he found her. She was pure and inspiring, with her profundity of thought and feeling. Loving her was like holding an angel from heaven.

Steven remembers how she encouraged his lost youthful idealism with her spiritual understanding. However, Steven was set in his perspective: Money makes the world go round. He was almost won over by this newfound love that made his heart beat faster and made him feel ten years younger. Almost.

Initially, Steven even moved to her small hometown, Normandale, spending a magical year with her. He felt great until he had a call from a business acquaintance who bragged about amassing greater wealth through his real estate and stock investments than Steven had ever achieved. Being competitive, Steven couldn't tolerate Roger outdoing him, when he was the one who taught him everything he knew.

He was fuming. When Diane asked him what was wrong, he replied: "My Company's stock is shooting up. If you have ever considered investing, now is the time. You'll make a killing! What do you say?"

"I don't know," Diane has replied. "I know next to nothing about stocks and I'm concerned because this is my entire retirement savings. If I lose this money, I won't have anything in my old age."

"Oh, you don't need to worry! You trust me right?"

"Well, of course I do. To me your love matters more than all the wealth in the world."

"Then don't give it a second thought. Invest everything you have in my company's stock and you won't regret it."

Even then Steven knew that what he was doing was illegal but he thought no one would catch on. His company's falsely inflated value would never be found out. He would make a killing, as he could take his fortune before anyone realised the real value of his stock. Yet, events didn't unfold according to plan; the federal authorities found out and arrested Steven. He lost his company. But thanks to his corrupt lawyers, he avoided incarceration and was only given a modest fine.

Steven didn't have any regrets about the whole fiasco. His brief period of change when he first met Diane was eclipsed by his strong greed for money. Sometimes he did wonder what happened to her, yet his priority remained financial gain at all costs. Yet, he often thought of her on many lonely nights and he wanted to call her. But, he couldn't. He had made a choice and it was a logical choice — a choice that would see him "succeed" with a lot of money, power and respect... but without love.

Steven sees the blank page staring at him and forcing him to write something. He scribbles with emotion: "Well, yes I loved. But, I've made my decision and it'll help me succeed."

He feels annoyed at the question because it brought to awareness questions that he wanted to remain buried. So he agitatedly throws the paper and pen at Chandra's feet and shouts, "There you have my answer!"

Chandra only smiles sympathetically and remains silent for a long period. Eventually, he picks up the paper and reads it, and then he remarks: "Success, my friend, can be measured at many levels. Sometimes, success in one area comes at the expense of something even more important. It's really a question of what you value. Some people value money more than love. Knowing what you value is important because fulfillment or happiness can only come when we can share our successes and even frustrations with others. We can make the way to the top a lonely journey but it doesn't have to be so."

For the first time, Steven is absolutely quiet at the retreat. For that brief moment he discerns Chandra's words. Then his intellect asserts itself with vehemence and he defensively thinks to himself: *Ha! A bunch of nonsense! Money is the foundation of everything. The real value of a person and society is the wealth they have and keep.*

Perceiving Steven's resistance, Chandra asserts: "Remember that change and continuity are two sides of the same coin. Life flows with its own rhythm and we cannot always control it wilfully. We have to allow for spontaneity as love can captivate us. It can make us take risks, but this is okay. Certain risks must be taken, if life is to be lived joyfully with vitality and excitement. A bank account, no matter how large, cannot fulfil our deepest longings for affection and communion with another soul and with other beings."

Chandra clears his throat and informs: "I must have spoken a lot and my throat is getting dry. So I'm going inside for a glass of water. Would you care to join me and continue our discussion?"

"No, thanks!" Steven snaps. "I'll think it over."

"Please do and whenever you feel like talking, just let me know," Chandra replies with a warm smile.

Meanwhile in another part of the room, Celeste asks Logan for a favour: "Would you do something for me?"

"What is it?" Logan asks, feeling unmotivated to carry out any requests.

"Will you walk to the top of the hill on the other side of the stream and find a medicinal herb for Muriel? She's having trouble sleeping at night, due extreme pain. This herb grows abundantly on the hilltop about three miles from here. The herb will ease her pain and help her get a good night's sleep. Will you do this for her?"

Logan is genuinely fond of Muriel yet is faced with inner turmoil when Celeste presents her request.

"What's wrong with her?" Logan asks.

Celeste explains: "She wants to keep it a secret for now. She really doesn't want to trouble anyone."

"I don't know. I'm not sure," he says. Logan really wants to help but feels he can't. In fact, he really doesn't feel like doing anything. Besides, going up a hill doesn't sound easy. He doesn't feel like battling with any obstacle, whether it's Mount Everest or just a tiny hill. *Muriel is a great woman, but if I feel so tired and upset, I shouldn't even try. Celeste doesn't realize how difficult this task is for me. I can imagine how each step of those three miles to the hill will be excruciatingly difficult. The hot sun would be beating down on me. Then, I'd get to that enormous hill and that would drain the remaining strength out of me...*

After another moment's reflection, Logan responds with a resolute, "No!"

"Why not?"

"Well, I just can't."

"Why can't you?"

"I'm not motivated."

"What keeps you from being motivated?"

"I'm just too tired, too exhausted. Basically, I'm just a hopeless case. I wasn't even able to hand in my reports on time at work."

"So, you feel that you are a hopeless case?"

"Yes!"

"Have you always been hopeless?"

"Well, no."

"Then, how can you identify yourself with a permanent label of being hopeless when at times you have shown yourself to be resourceful in the past. Since you have been resourceful in the past, then you can be so now. Isn't that so?"

"Yeah, I guess so."

"What seems to be keeping you immobilized is your label that you're hopeless and because you feel you are hopeless, you stop trying. When you don't try, you feel even more miserable and hopeless. It becomes a self-fulfilling tragedy."

After a long time, Logan begins to feel glimmers of hope. His doubts start to leave him as he gains a belief in his capabilities. To confirm these positive feelings, he requests: "Could you expand on what you said, Celeste?"

"Sure, Logan. It's like this: If you put motivation before action, then you will continue to wait until you feel motivated. On the other hand, if you take action, then the motivation will surely follow."

"Okay; that sounds good but I have depression. I can't control how I feel."

"We can discuss your feelings another time. Why don't you take action now, and then evaluate how you feel. Go to the hill and get the herb for Muriel."

"Okay, I'll give it a try. I really like Muriel and I do want to help her. Point me to the hill."

"That's the spirit!" Celeste enthusiastically cries as she points to the far off hill and gives him a description of the medicinal herb as he leaves: "You're looking for a plant that grows about 2 meters high. It has creamy white flowers growing together into a rounded cluster or umbel like Queen's Anne Lace. It's an unmistakable plant and you'll easily spot it. Good luck on your journey!"

Logan begins his journey as he waves goodbye to Celeste in the distance. When he starts walking, he begins to notice that getting his body in motion does lift his mental fog. He starts feeling less dejected and even somewhat enthusiastic. The sun doesn't seem unbearable, especially as a cool breeze plays with his hair. He reflects on Celeste's words. She was right: Now that he is taking action, he does feel better.

After 20 minutes, Logan notices he does feel more motivated, but the journey is only a third complete. He looks off into the distance. He sees the hill. With that sight, he regains his momentum. Simultaneously his negative thoughts disappear like nocturnal creatures that become inactive with daylight.

Logan starts to see his journey as an adventure. He feels like an explorer trekking his way through the wilderness with only his tenacity and intuition as guides. He will triumph like a mythic hero, bringing back the prize: Muriel's medicinal herb.

While in these thoughts of optimism and grandeur the next forty minutes pass, Logan reaches the hill more quickly than he had anticipated. *Wow! That wasn't so bad.*

As Logan stands at the bottom of the hill he gazes up to the top, feeling somewhat concerned at its immense height. But, he reminds himself how far he has already come. He hears Celeste's voice: "Remember action before motivation." As he remembers her words, he feels that he can do it. He can scale the hill and it should take him no more than fifteen to twenty minutes to walk to the top, and so without another moment's hesitation the next leg of his journey begins.

A scent of wild roses fills the air as Logan walks along the path. Birds sing, melodious and free. Their tune carries him along with greater ease. Butterflies playfully dance as they flutter amongst the flowers. One butterfly lands on Logan's shoulder and he feels encouraged, as if this is a good sign.

Logan begins to walk swiftly but always carefully maintaining his footing.

The scenery is so beautiful around him that he looses all sense of time. Then, he remembers to keep moving his body. As he does so his motivation increases. With newly discovered motivation, his energy becomes more charged. Logan begins to realize that the climb is not nearly as difficult as he had imagined.

Suddenly Logan stops abruptly. From out of nowhere a diminutive, white bearded man appears, carrying a large staff.

Logan is so startled that he veers back off the path and falls over the edge of a dangerously steep cliff.

He luckily grasps onto the edge of the cliff, with his bandaged hands and holds on for dear life. His struggle to hold on is intense. He fears that if he loses his grip he may not survive the fall.

"Who are you?" the white bearded man asks.

"I'm Logan," he gasps while trembling.

"No, who are you really?" the man insists.

"Alright, then if I'm not Logan, then who am I?" Logan cries trembling with fear, as tears and sweat run profusely down his face, his shirt drenched.

"Ah, now you've asked the key question. 'Who am I?'" smiles the man.

"I don't care who I am or who you are. Help me before I fall! I can't hold on much longer!" Logan pleads fervently.

"Oh, no. Why is it that the most simple is often the most difficult to find?" continues the old man. He seems lost in his own riddle, unaware of Logan's predicament.

"Help me, please. Help!" Logan is terrified, barely able to hold on another moment.

Suddenly, the white bearded man holds out his staff and says: "Here, hold on to this."

One hand at a time, Logan grasps onto the staff. The old man effortlessly pulls him up onto a grassy area beside the path. Logan moans in relief, rubbing his sore hands that are now irritated even further. The pain is excruciating. The old man takes some pieces of a plant out of his pocket. He rubs the succulent leaves gently on Logan's hands as he explains that the aloe-vera leaves will help accelerate the healing and ease the painful sensations. Logan is surprised when he finds that the pain is instantly relieved.

"Amazing," declares Logan. "And how did you manage to pull me up when I weigh much more than you?"

The old man obliviously continues talking as Logan recovers from his ordeal: "You are not just your body, mind, senses, or name. You are the Eternal True Self. When you were falling off the cliff, you were frightened because you equated your self as synonymous with your body. Yet, even if your body composed of five elements becomes extinguished, you will still live on."

With that, the old man points his staff up into the air and brings it down with a heavy thud on the ground to emphasize his point. "You are the miracle of life and you have unlimited potential. You are light, love, and energetic motion and stillness. Remember who you are! Do not see yourself in a static mould, you are "being" even in motion. To define or label yourself narrowly is not to understand the depth of your own self. To believe 'I can't' is an illusion, but to believe 'I'll try' is to recognize you have no limit. Be free from setting narrow boundaries on yourself. Remember to first take action, and then even the impossible is possible" the old man reiterates passionately.

"Wow," declares Logan! "That's just what Celeste told me."

"She is a wise woman, this Celeste," the old man says with absolute confidence as if he knows her well. "My name is Sunny but I'll have to go now. Good luck on your journey." Then just as swiftly as he had appeared, the man turns and leaves, wandering out of sight behind trees off in the distance.

Logan sits there, more perplexed than ever. He wonders if the man was real or just imaginary. He considers that too much sun can lead to hallucinating. Regardless, the tiny old man was interesting and his words profound.

After a moment, Logan decides that instead of just sitting there bewildered he must make his body move and then perhaps his motivation to reach the top of the hill will return. He steadily places one foot in front of the next. Then as his motivation returns, Logan is thankful for the extra burst of energy that helps him reach the top. When he gazes around he notices that the medicinal herb is growing everywhere. Happy to find the plant so easily, and in such abundance, he fills his backpack with the herb. Now he feels like a real hero. He enjoys the feeling of strength in having achieved a successful climb to the top of the hill.

Logan stops for a moment to view the wondrous scenery. Lavender and white wild flowers grow tall and profusely, as they joyously dance in the breeze. He listens intently, and hears the wind singing among trees. Logan is in awe of such a profound experience, yet goes with the flow. He feels elated, blissful, and serene. Every aspect of his being is in stillness, as he listens to this Universal Symphony — a symphony of more than just the wind but the entire universe in movement. He is captivated with the wonder of a paradox; directly experiencing, by means of his five senses, what is beyond his five senses. He effortlessly feels expanded consciousness and while doing so gazes at his surroundings. Wild roses are growing freely throughout the hilltop. Daylilies add a splash of colour throughout the surroundings, with their yellows, oranges, and golden hues.

He turns his gaze and finds two butterflies playfully chasing one another, flying in and out amongst the lilies. The sky is a most brilliant blue, and overflowing with billowing, soft white clouds that drift lazily along. Two doves are nestled in a nearby blue spruce tree, and coo back and forth with each other. A humming bird discovers some nectar from a honey suckle bush and hovers there contentedly.

Logan perceives the paradox of stillness in the motion while viewing the movements of bountiful nature and the simultaneous motion in the stillness, as indiscernible forces like the elements will create change over time of epochs.

The experience lovingly touches the depths of his heart. He ponders about how the mystical is magically interwoven within nature.

Logan feasts his eyes on more of the natural beauty surrounding him. The wisteria forms an archway, as it grows intertwined, full with deep rich flowers.

Some wild strawberries are amongst the daisies, Queen-Anne's Lace and wild buttercups. Logan considers that perhaps he could live here forever; it's a real paradise.

However, there is a "call" in his heart that determines his place is to be back with the group at the retreat. Why? So that his dream, his life purpose may unfold. He senses, without a doubt, that it is time for him to leave. He also realizes that he is intertwined with the entire cosmos as an integral part of this natural Universal masterpiece. After enjoying the wonders of the hilltop for a while he is ready for his descent back to the group. He journeys down the hill with ease.

Logan walks beside his companion, the winding stream, once again and enjoys the sound of the flowing water as it trickles around some rocks. The water is clear and reflects the pinks of the setting sun. The stream has an energy and vitality to it that harmonizes so perfectly with the earth of the meadows, the air of the sky and the fire of the sun. Logan reflects on how all things are connected. He directly experiences the presence of Universal harmony.

It feels soothing, healing to notice the beauty of his surroundings. He feels especially attracted to the stream. The flowing water has a high energy. He takes off his shoes and stands with his bare feet in the stream and is soothed by its flow. The water rushes by, harmonious, yet energized and powerful. Logan contemplates how he would like to be as "flowing" as the stream. Then he steps out of the water, and, after putting on his shoes, continues his walk, refreshed and rejuvenated. He arrives back at the old stone house at dusk to find Celeste waiting for him.

"How was it Logan? Did you make it to the top?" Celeste curiously asks.

"It was easier than I had anticipated" Logan says, as he opens his backpack to show Celeste the medicinal herb.

"Yes, that's it, wonderful. Thank you, kindly" Celeste says, as she looks deep into Logan's eyes, and inquires: "Did it work? If you moved your body first did your motivation soon follow?"

"Surprisingly, it did. At the beginning I was thinking about giving up. I really had to force myself to keep going. Then, much to my astonishment I did feel motivated very soon afterwards. I was really surprised but it worked. Not near as impossible as I had imagined," he remarks.

Then he helps Celeste to place the medicinal herb in her large canvas bag.

"I'm so happy and this will be of such help for Muriel. She suffers more than she lets on, you know," informs Celeste.

"I didn't know. I hope the herb will relieve her suffering,"

Logan says. As he places his empty backpack on his shoulder, he looks toward Celeste.

"I'm wondering about something," Logan confides. "Do you know of a little white bearded man, with a huge staff, who is up on the hill?" he queries, looking inquisitively at Celeste.

"I'm not sure who you're talking about," Celeste replies. "You know some things in life will always remain a mystery. That's just the way it is."

Celeste holds some of the medicinal herbs in her hands and concludes: "Logan you have demonstrated great compassion today. I realize that it must have been a challenge. Dr. Karl Menninger once said that 'Love cures people — both the ones who give it and the ones who receive it.' It's not just the herb but the love shown in obtaining it that helps with healing."

"Celeste, why do you do all this?" You could just retire and do nothing the rest of your life. Why all this?" asks Logan.

"I want to be of help, even if it's only for a few people and only in a small way. If I can somehow ease suffering, then I will be content," Celeste affirms.

Logan looks at Celeste for a moment then smiles silently. He knows she is deeply sincere.

"It's appreciated," he asserts. "I learned something today, something that I'll always remember. It is of great significance and it really works...

"Move my body first and then the motivation will follow," Logan adds thoughtfully.

Celeste instructively notes: "The mystic journey is all about discovering your heart in ever deepening ways. Belief has a great impact in overcoming doubt. It's not easy to believe, for doubt and hopelessness can easily sway the mind and heart but with trust belief can refashion your concepts. Just be open and accept this change with gratitude."

Everyone gathers back in the old stone house. The wood is crackling in the fireplace to warm the cool chill of the evening. Chandra invites each person to find a place in the circle once again.

"I've been thinking about our friends Stephen and Logan," he states. "After some reviewing what they wrote, I have something that I would like to say to both of them; however my thoughts may also be beneficial to everyone in our circle."

"My words are few but may help you along the way throughout your life. Be of good character. Help to lift one another up and in so doing, perhaps transform your own lives as well. After all what is life for? We're born, we live, and then we die. We are a moment in life's eternal song. Help to lift one another up."

A pause, and then: "In so doing, be like a steady candle flame, not like a flickering flame. Have steadiness. Wisdom reveals that it is Love that gives us the energy to sustain us along the path. It is Love that sustains us, for money is ephemeral. True Love is eternal, passionate, energized and sustaining. Choose your path with wisdom. All I can say is if you choose to walk along the path of Love, it is always a path full of roses, but as with roses you can sometimes be pricked by thorns," Chandra enlightens.

Logan remarks: "Chandra, today I journeyed to the hill gathering a medicinal herb and I realized something from my adventure. The impossible is possible. I grasp this but believing and truly knowing is different than surface understanding."

Chandra nodded agreement: "It takes time before knowledge is assimilated and engenders convictions, beliefs and principles for life. You have begun the journey and each step you take will offer you experience — experience that will sometimes be pleasant and at other times unpleasant. You will have aromatic fragrance of roses but thorns will also prick you, so that you can experience the totality of life. You have to accept everything on the path of Love. Even if it is despair, loneliness or anguish because these too are Divine gifts. They are also part of your growth. When we reject these troubling aspects of life, we are rejecting essential aspects of a commonly shared human experience."

Logan looks puzzled with a wrinkled brow. "I'm troubled Chandra. If this is what walking the path of love is all about, then I've lost all hope."

He thinks of Sarah, and then continues: "I've learned something today but I don't know if I have the strength to deal with the cruelty of life. Before I could but now I'm broken —

broken inside. I often feel empty, cold like a candle without a flame."

Chandra considers Logan's comments, and then advises: "Remember steadiness—be like the steady candle-flame, Logan. Walk with wisdom and don't let your mind be troubled by doubts, fears and hurts. Chose to walk along the path of Love even when you don't always receive the object of your desires."

"I need to tough if out sometimes," Logan suggests.

Chandra nods agreement: "If we were guaranteed to receive an abundance of security, love and joy in steady supply, would there be sincerity in what we do or the choice we make? To choose love means just that; to choose love with all its ups and downs, gains and losses. Continue walking on the path of love."

"So," Logan considers, "the path isn't always pleasant, but it's important to keep focused on it..."

"Yes, never forget to be like the steady candle flame, which requires a steady mind, not the flickering candle-flame where the mind easily oscillates. The 'flickering flame' can also be on the path of love, yet it often questions love's validity; it often changes paths as mental, emotional and spiritual doubts plague it. It oscillates: love then fear, love then fear. Your highest good will manifest all in Divine time. Be steadiness."

"What if I waver or 'flicker' sometimes? Logan asks. "How important is it to always believe in this path?"

"Know that you walk in universal harmony when you walk on the path of love; walk with trust and complete belief. Know this with your every breath, with all of your heart, mind, body and soul. Know this with every beat of your heart. If you ever feel unsteady while walking along the path of love, just ask yourself 'what is the loving thing to do?' Then your clarity and steadiness will be restored. Know that love, and all of your highest good will is guaranteed, all in Divine time."

Chandra completes his ideas of Love with a quote: "Logan, remember this to help maintain equanimity. As Henry Van Dyke once said 'Time is too slow for those who want, too swift for those who fear, too long for those who grieve, too short for those who rejoice, but for those who love, time is eternity.' "

Everyone is thoughtful as they ponder Chandra's reflections

on love, especially Logan. Some precious moments of silence surround everyone. Soon Celeste begins to conclude the evening with a story: "In India, a high government official, Malik Bhago, once invited Guru Nanak while on his journey to attend his feast. But, Guru Nanak stayed instead at the home of a poor carpenter, Bhai Lalo, who earned his money by honest work. Guru Nanak shared in his coarse bread instead of Malik Bhago's feast earned through exploitation of others. Malik Bhago was persistent and asked a second time. So the Guru took Bhai Lalo with him to the official's home. With great anger Malik Bhago said to Guru Nanak: 'You are dishonouring the high caste by eating dry chapattis in the house of a low caste carpenter. My feast will offer you delicious food. Why do you refuse to eat it?'"

Celeste paused for effect, then continued: "Guru Nanak took Bhai Lalo's dry chapatti in his right hand and Malik Bhago's fried bread in his left hand. When he squeezed the right hand the people present there saw drops of milk dripping from it. When he pressed the left hand with the Malik Bhago's fried pancakes, everyone saw blood trickling from it. The Guru uttered: 'Look Malik Bhago, wealth gathered by cruelty towards the poor is like sucking their blood, which you have done. You had invited me to partake of blood, leaving food pure as milk. How could I accept it?' So according to Guru Nanak it's better to earn little money with honesty than to amass wealth by devious and crooked means."

Then, Chandra reads another story of Guru Nanak from a book to close the evening's discussion: "Guru Nanak and Mardana, his faithful companion, continued to travel. One day, they arrived near Lahore. The Guru decided to stay outside the city. He sat on a grassy spot near the river Ravi. Sitting there, he fixed his thoughts on God. Mardana sang the Guru devotional songs. Sometimes, the Guru himself would begin to sing them. Soon people began to gather around Guru Nanak. They liked the singing and the Guru's talks. One day, a rich man of Lahore came to him. He asked him to visit his house. The Guru replied, "I am all right here. I am not fond of grand houses. Moreover, my visit to your house might cause you some trouble." But Duni Chand repeated his request, again and again…"

Chandra reaches for a glass of water, and continues a moment later: "The Guru agreed, at last, to go with him to his house. On reaching there, the Guru saw a number of flags flying on Duni Chand's house. He smiled on seeing the flags. Duni Chand took the Guru and Mardana inside the house. He gave them good food to eat. He gave them cool water to drink. Then he sat near the Guru, with folded hands. After a time, the Guru asked, "The number of flags that are flying on your roof, what do they mean?" Duni Chand replied: "They are to show how much wealth I have. Every flag represents 10 million rupees. I have total of seven flags." The Guru said, "Then you are a very rich man. But are you happy and satisfied?" "Holy sir, I must not lie to you. Some people are much richer than I. This makes me desire more and more. I want to be the richest man in the country. I cannot feel happy and satisfied until my desire is fulfilled," Duni Chand replied."

Another sip of water, and Chandra resumed the story-telling: "Guru Nanak then observed: "But the people richer than you must also be trying to become richer and richer. Thus, there is a race between them and you. Perhaps, you may not be able to beat them in this race for wealth. You may, therefore, never be happy. Have you ever thought of that?" Duni Chand seemed puzzled: "Holy Sir, I have no time to think such thoughts." Guru Nanak smiled and said, "Will you have time to do a small thing for me?" Duni Chand replied, "Most gladly, sir. What can I do for you?" The Guru took out a needle, and instructed, "Please keep it with you. Give it to me, when I ask for it, in the next world."

Chandra smiles. "There's more: Duni Chand took the needle to his wife. He gave it to her and explained: "The holy man wants us to keep the needle for him. He will take it back from us in the next world." She said. "Are you mad? How can a needle go to the next world? How can we carry it with us there? Go back, and return it to the holy man." Duni Chand went back to the Guru and said, "Master, take back your needle. It cannot go with me to the next world. I cannot carry it there." The Guru smiled and said, "The needle is small and light. You say that it cannot go with you to the next world. How then can your vast wealth go there with you? What good can it do to you there?" Duni Chand fell at the Guru's feet and said, "Tell me how my wealth may go with me to the next world." The Guru said, "Give it to the poor in the name of God. Feed the hungry. Clothe the naked. Help the needy. What you spend thus will go with you in the next world." Duni Chand accepted this advice. He gave away all his wealth to the poor. What he gave away in wealth he gained in spiritual fulfillment. He and his wife experienced true satisfaction that remained elusive from them by merely amassing wealth."

Chandra concludes: "We can elaborate on the meaning of these stories, but that would keep you from reflecting upon them and making them personally relevant for you. These stories are great bedtime stories and I can see from many of your expressions and yawns that they have been successful. So, let's call it a night. I'll put out the candles, and wish everyone enchanting dreams."

As everyone begins to leave, Sarah turns to Logan: "Listen, about yesterday, it's all forgiven but don't ever do it again!"

"I know and I'm sorry. It won't happen again," Logan replies sombrely. His positive feelings are hard to sustain when he remembers how foolishly he'd acted yesterday.

Indeed, even though Logan had experienced a positive mood and motivation while climbing the hill earlier on in the day, the remembrance of his previous night's rage throws him into another bout of melancholia.

Logan places his hands in his pockets, and with head hung low turns to walk away alone. Perhaps within the depths of his being there exists a deep, dark sorrow — a sorrow that is buried so deep that it is almost imperceptible. Yet, it surfaces in his conscious awareness on occasion, briefly yet with force.

"Hey Logan" calls Steven, slowly limping with his cane "wasn't that a joke? Just think, all that talk about sincerity and compassion. Ha! The only people that want compassion are the people on the 'bottom'; you know the one's that have no money. Well, compassion sounds nice in a story, but in real life? People respond to power and influence, not kindness. Compassion is too weak to earn respect from them."

Logan doesn't even bother to listen to Steven. He just continues walking, fatigued, perplexed and feeling alone.

Steven walks away to retire for the evening and reflects loudly on some of the evening's discussion. "Two sides of the same coin?" he ruminates. "The only coins I care about are the ones I can save in my bank account. Now those coins are worth something. At least I can do something with them and make a real difference in my life."

Chandra overhears and calls out to Stephen: "My friend, peace of mind is real happiness. That was the key point of tonight's stories. We can't look for satisfaction only in objects because they can't satisfy until we feel an inner contentment."

"I will be truly happy," Steven retorts, "when my back heals, and then I can begin my next venture... it's a sure multi-million dollar scheme."

"That's why I'm here," he adds. "Spirituality can be marketed and you can make a lot of money from it. I'm going to cash in on it," declares Steven as he waves his cane in the air. He falls to the ground and irritates his back injury even further. "Oh! Would you help me up? I just lost my balance."

"Now there's where we agree," laughs Chandra as he helps Steven to his feet: "There you go, you should be alright now. I have to go for some much needed sleep so I'll see you later. If you have any problem with your back, you can call me but you will also find some Aspirin on the bedside table. Can you manage on your own?"

"Yes, I'm okay, but thanks for the offer," Steven utters with some discomfort as he hobbles to his cabin.

"The only balance that really matters to me is the balance in my bank account and that will be doing fine soon, so I'll be happy again," Stephen mutters.

"You have the answer on achieving happiness have you?" Chandra inquires, while whistling a tune, as he begins to walk away.

Time is too slow for those who want, too swift for those who fear, too long for those who grieve, too short for those who rejoice, but for those who love, time is eternity.

- Henry Van Dyke

6

The Circle of Life

The past two weeks had been exceedingly difficult for Logan even though his hands had healed within that time, except for a scar that ran beside his left thumb.

The bandages were removed and he felt cheerful for the first few weeks, however his sense of loneliness had increased.

That loneliness became worse when he noticed that Sarah had been increasingly avoiding him. Even when he smiled, she would just turn away. Logan wanted to develop at least a friendship with her. He made repeated gestures, yet each time she wouldn't even acknowledge his presence. Her coldness really upset him.

Logan had asked her, "Sarah, am I invisible to you? Why are you being so cold to me?"

"I don't have time for this," Sarah tersely replied, and then turned around and walked away, leaving Logan totally confused.

That incident and the other times he had suffered her rejections really hurt him. Soon the hurt turned back to dejection with loneliness following in its footsteps.

Yet, Logan had finally felt hope at the retreat. The insights at the retreat offered by Celeste and Chandra were making him feel positive about the future. He was starting to develop an awareness of the pain he was carrying with him instead of staying in denial. Most importantly, he was creating new beliefs about himself ever since his climb to the top of the hill; instead of remaining paralyzed by hopelessness and doubt.

But now, his progress had been reversed. Whatever inner progress he had made was now swallowed by the dark shadows of hopelessness, sadness and loneliness.

For the next two days, the weather became ugly, overcast with dark, ominous clouds and a build up of atmospheric pressure and winds. During one night, the clouds break as Logan walks back to his cottage in torrential rain and with mighty gusts of wind. Branches are stripped from trees.

Logan dashes into his cottage and strips off his wet clothes, putting on some dry, comfortable ones. He sits down in front of his window, looking at the lightning show outside. He sees a distant flash as the lightning strikes a mighty tree and then he hears a loud roar that shakes the ground. As the lightning flashes once more, Logan's face otherwise surrounded by darkness is lit for just a moment. He looks pale and concerned. His sense of loneliness and despondency is increased with the lack of sunshine. With the rain, Logan wants even more to have Sarah beside him, but instead he falls asleep alone, listening to the dripping of water outside as the rain shower ends.

The next few days are a total contrast to the rainy weather before with hot, humid temperatures. Logan enjoys the sunshine but the intense heat makes him feel apathetic. After two days of heat, Logan is woken with the sun shimmering through branches, the light dancing on his face. He is drenched in sweat from another sweltering summer night; so he relaxes in bed not wanting to move.

Then, abruptly he hears a knock on his cabin door followed by Chandra's voice: "Logan, I have a task for you to complete. Meet the others and me at the stone house in fifteen minutes. Can I count on you to be there?"

"Yes, I'll be there. I just need to get dressed. See you, soon."

"Very good!" Chandra replies before leaving.

Logan gets dressed. He welcomes having something to do.

Since, the journey to the hill, he notices that when he absorbs himself in a task, he feels better but when he mopes around, he feels worse. He is ready to go, and arrives at the stone-house five minutes before everyone else.

Logan feels proud of this accomplishment, realizing that he can get moving even with negative emotions. Often when he experienced dark thoughts, he would want to sulk and remain isolated from others. The climb up the hill was a turning point for him. It showed him that with a little effort, he could accomplish tasks even when his mind told him it's impossible. His belief could dispel doubts and feelings of hopelessness. Those beliefs were best changed by personal accomplishments, which reinforced positive self-image over negative thoughts and emotions.

Yet, his greatest vulnerability remained Sarah and ever since she started to snub him, he regressed into the cycle of negative emotions. He doubted whether he could make any further progress now.

Logan also realized he had no one with whom he could relate. No one would understand the depths of his soul. The only person who intimately knew him, Sarah, couldn't be relied on any more. She proved that when she turned to Kurt and now her coldness revealed all too clearly her lack of consideration for his feelings. Clearly, not even Sarah knew his heart; how much he agonized and suffered. Only he knew his pain—his loneliness.

His thoughts are interrupted, as he feels a tap on his shoulder and then hears Chandra's soothing voice.

"Well, Logan, you're the first to arrive. Great! It'll give us a chance to speak together. You know, Logan, Celeste confided in me that you have depression. I hope you don't mind her telling me?"

"No, I don't. I never asked her to keep it a secret but I don't want it advertised to everyone."

"We wouldn't do that. She only told me because she thought I could help."

"Well, I'm not sure if you can help."

"You might be right. Still, can we talk as friends?"

"Sure, why not?"

"Celeste also told me that since the journey to the hill, you've found the secret to motivation."

"Yes, I did. You don't wait around for motivation. You take action and the motivation comes as you get moving," Logan proudly declares.

"Excellent! You've mastered an important lesson. Now, I've also heard that something is troubling you. Would you share with me what distresses you?"

"Well, it's hard to say and I don't know if you would understand."

"Try me. I'm a great listener."

"I know but you don't experience what I feel."

"You mean due to your depression?"

"Yes, plus I can't deal with the disappointments in my life, particularly when an important person has let me down. I've been depressed since my losses last year. I don't know if I can ever feel whole because my depression has defeated me."

"Logan, I have something to share with you. I have also had serious depression about twenty years ago. I call it depression but what I experienced was different than clinical depression."

"What do you mean?"

"You see I had a spiritual problem not a biological problem, such as, a chemical imbalance which distorts your thinking. It's a fine distinction. The difference is that depression's root cause is the chemistry of the brain, while despair is a spiritual malady that originates from a deep, gnawing feeling of brokenness, isolation and uncanny sensitivity to the world and its problems. The root cause of despair is feeling disconnected from everyone around you. It can be healed by re-establishing a sense of community, harmony and integrity. Does that make sense?"

"No, not really."

"Okay, then allow me to explain it further. Ultimately despair is created by the mind and the answer to healing it lays also in the mind — in creating a steady mind. Have you been on anti-depressants?"

"Yes."

"And you didn't stop taking them?"

"No, I have continued to take them but they haven't helped."

"In that case, trying other approaches is a sensible idea. The main thing is not to give up hope, or to start believing you can't be helped. Any challenge can have many dimensions to it. Therefore, to correct it, you have to be open to different approaches. Often times, medication along with therapy for some people is more helpful than drugs alone, especially when the problems may be rooted in more than just a chemical imbalance in the brain."

"That sounds nice but I can't see overcoming my depression or despair for good."

"Logan, I've gone through this same phase myself. It was so bad that I felt hopeless. I couldn't see myself getting out of it either. Some days I would feel so bad that I didn't want to get out of bed. My body ached and I lost interest in everything that I liked before. I even started to lose weight. What really shook me were my suicidal thoughts. I felt nothing would change; I would always suffer. So, suicide seemed like a logical choice. If it would never end, why not end it?"

"You?" Logan asks incredulously, "you felt that way? I can't believe it. You're so spiritual; so together."

"Having these feelings doesn't make you unspiritual. You may sometimes feel worthless because you have a tendency to undervalue yourself. Sometimes when you're down, you can feel you're going insane, or that you're falling apart. However, this is normal when your thoughts and feelings are influenced by despair or depression. You may even feel special, since you're able to see the world realistically, not through rose-colored glasses like everyone else. Nevertheless, all these are mental distortions. You don't see reality objectively; it becomes very much a subjective experience. Your distorted thoughts make you see reality through the lens of hopelessness, and in turn reinforce your depressive emotions."

Logan sighs. "So what am I supposed to do about all this?"

"The first step to reclaiming your life is to practice conscious awareness of your mental and emotional states instead of being in denial about them. Are they working for your benefit? Or, are distortions clouding your understanding? Hurt, fear and anger can distort the mind, throw our emotions into chaos, and leave tensions in our body."

"I'm feeling all of that," Logan acknowledges, "big time."

"Yoga such as the postures we have practiced, meditation like the times we have stilled the mind by focusing on our breath and visualization like the forgiveness exercise – they're all great aids to our growth. In this way we can take ownership of our life and release these negative feelings, as we prepare our heart for forgiveness both of our unskilled actions and those of others who have acted unkindly to us."

"How do we get to that point?" Logan asks.

"After conscious awareness and proving to ourselves that we do in fact need to make some important changes in our heart and mind, we start to evaluate our beliefs and assumptions, especially self-beliefs and labels in order to evaluate whether they are beneficial or detrimental for our growth. Then, a final step is necessary, which involves connecting to the Nexus within and to the Nexus outside."

"You have often mentioned this Nexus but what does it mean?" Logan inquires, somewhat bewildered.

"I'm glad you asked that. What do you think it means?"

"Well, Nexus means some sort of tie, a means of connection, or a link of some kind."

"Exactly!"

"But you mention an inner and outer Nexus."

"Yes, inner and outer are only for convenience as our language conventionally divides reality into discursive elements. Yet, if we view reality from an integrated perspective we would realize only wholeness. This is the Nexus and this Nexus is found within us when we intuitively sense the oneness of reality instead of exclusively recognizing its division into parts. The parts are there but so too is the wholeness. Does that make sense?"

"Well, sure, it makes some sense. What about the Nexus outside of us?"

"The Nexus inside connects to the Nexus outside through certain portals, the easiest portals for most people to access are empathy and compassion."

"Now I'm lost Chandra. It made sense up until that point."

"I know it sounds complicated when it really isn't. Rather than explaining it, what we are planning today will experientially reinforce the importance of compassion."

Logan pensively nods his assent, somewhat excited about today's adventure. He adds with a smile: "Are you going to have us try levitation today?"

Chandra chuckles and then he states: "Logan, I don't just know what you're experiencing theoretically but I have actually lived through it, and I can tell you there is hope even when everything seems dark and oppressive. You will again feel joy. You will not be condemned to feeling hopeless, worthless and lonely forever."

"Once you realize how intimately all of life is interconnected, then your sorrow will not be an isolated occurrence of sorrow. It will become the portal through which compassion enters your heart. This portal leads to the Nexus that connects all beings. Through compassion and empathy; we can connect to beings around us. Once that connection, that Nexus, is realized both within us and outside us; then personal isolation and loneliness give way to a true feeling of involvement in all life. Then, the walls of hurt and anger will yield to forgiveness, acceptance and courage. It's the kind of courage that allows you to love and to live life to the fullest."

Logan isn't convinced he should believe Chandra's words since they seem chimerical. Yet he's developed a deep trust with his teacher, so he asks: "What do you mean, exactly?"

"When you're in the valley of despair, you are suspicious of anyone declaring to you from the mountaintop that you will feel better because your feelings tell you otherwise. Your hopelessness asserts that you will always be hopeless. But, you know, feelings like thoughts are never permanent. They're like shadows cast by swiftly moving clouds. The shadows exist yet they arise and subside; therefore their reality is conditional. They're temporal. They arise and subside. Thoughts and feelings are only temporally real. They are not permanent fixtures of your psyche. So, just watch them rise and fall, like the tides of the ocean. Just as clouds drift by casting shadows upon the ground, similarly negative emotions have their moment when they cast an oppressive shadow on your perception. Yet in time they are gone. Just be patient and realize their impermanence."

Logan ponders Chandra's words. They resonate within him and their truth soothes his mind like a balm.

Chandra then asks him directly: "What is troubling you, right now?"

Logan answers: "Loneliness."

"Ah, yes, loneliness. I know it all too well. You feel disconnected from others. You feel apart from reality, not a part of reality. You feel distant from people and you know that they can't possibly understand you. Does that sound right?"

"Yes, that's exactly what I feel."

"Then, our task today will be immensely helpful."

Just as Chandra finishes speaking, the rest of the group arrives to join them.

Steven can be overheard above everyone else: "Spirituality can really sell, Celeste. If you marketed this retreat well, you could make millions."

"A million would be nice, especially since it can be used for so much good. But, right now we're happy to be working with small groups. It's much more personal. Besides, we have all we need and we're content," Celeste replies.

Steven scratches his head completely perplexed by her comments. Sarah, who is getting irritated with Steven's talking, speaks up: "Shut up, Steven and let's enjoy our time here without discussion of money for a change!"

Taken aback by Sarah's outburst, Steven has no reply and decides to remain quiet — at least for now. But, he is certain that the others have no idea that money is what really matters in this world. He wonders if hanging around them would make him lose his drive and initiative.

Logan looks carefully at Sarah. She appears ravishingly seductive in her clinging tank top. If only he could hold her tightly and reveal his love for her. He yearns for her, and can feel his heart racing just looking at her. Nothing would be more fulfilling than to reconnect with her and to share with her moments of laughter, conversation and exhilarating touch. Why on earth was she with this... *Kurt*? He couldn't possibly love her the way he did? Logan feels like going up to Sarah and just telling her to drop Kurt and to be with him. It made perfect sense to him, so why can't Sarah see it?

Even with all these thoughts, Logan knows that the moment for them may have forever passed in the progression of time. Besides, Sarah behaved rudely and he couldn't forgive her abuse. At the very least, she could just try being nice to him – that wasn't too much to ask. But she is too engrossed in her conversation with Muriel to even notice him. So he clamps down on his passions, feeling annoyed for loving her so much and exasperated with her for her surliness. He is again reminded of the depth of his loneliness and isolation.

Chandra interrupts Logan's thoughts with his announcement: "The weather has been extremely hot and dry. We had days of rain, wind and thunder that knocked down a massive tree."

As Chandra speaks of a tree knocked down by lightning, Logan remembers seeing it from his cabin's window during the rainstorm.

Chandra continues: "We have smouldering sunshine now"

Sarah concurs: "You're not kidding. It's incredibly hot and sticky."

"Yes, I know the weather is uncomfortable and I really thank everyone for coming out today in this heat. The hot sun has also soaked up any still water. So, I would like everyone to follow me. I want to show you something."

Chandra begins to walk away with his hiking stick as others follow him in a disorderly fashion. They feel tired with the heat but being in the group makes them feel adventurous. The grass around them is a light brown from the dry conditions and excessive heat. Waves of hazy steam can be seen in the air with the sun glaring down from its celestial abode. The mid-afternoon heat feels unbearable. Most of the group is wearing light clothing: shorts, T-shirts and tank tops to help them to cope with the heat.

A putrid smell fills the air. It reminds Logan of decay and death. Something is dead or dying and its foul stench is in the air. Sarah holds her nose and exclaims: "What is that awful smell?"

Chandra halts and begins to speak: "I apologize for bringing you out in such heat; however the heat is causing more suffering than you know. Let's walk a bit further and you'll understand what I mean."

They walk further. The air is filled with death. In front of them lies a pond, which is mostly mud now with a small amount of water in the center.

Just a month ago, a beautiful pond existed, filled with life and water. Now, the sun shimmers on the cesspool and glows on the floating bodies of dead fish. The whole pond eerily glistens with their silvery carcasses.

Logan shudders at the sight. Then, he hears splashing in front of him. A large fish, whose eyes seem to look directly at Logan, is encased in mud... madly struggles, gasping for air. It desperately attempts to breathe in the stagnant remnants of its watery abode. Suffocating, it slowly is dying. As Logan surveys the pool, he realizes that the struggle for survival is not only with this one fish but is common to the entire pond. Every living fish struggles for oxygen in the still, muddy pool. How will they survive? Their companions have lost the contest and their corpses float as reminders of how close death is to life.

Now, Logan feels a sense of overpowering empathy in his heart. In an instant, he connects to the struggle of the fish. He can feel its life ebbing away just as his own life had lost its vitality. Sensing its pain and loneliness, which are no different than his own, he gently touches the fish that is now still. In his mind, he can hear its heartbeat slowing, slowing and then stopping until the silence of the now becomes deafening. The fish gave up its struggle and in time it accepts the inevitable, death; then the struggle ends as its consciousness, vitality is finished. The circle of its life is completed. He had accompanied the creature in its final journey. He felt at one with the creature as his awareness expanded, as tenderness filled his heart. He is now filled with sorrow and resolutely asks himself: How can I rescue the remaining creatures from dying in this agony?

He feels a warm hand on his shoulder, which makes him shudder and then relax. "Logan, you showed compassion for it.

You accompanied it. There is beauty in comforting the dying," Chandra consoles, then he steps back and announces to the group: "I know this is a troubling sight but we can do something to renew this stagnant pond. We need to work together to complete the task at hand. We have to connect this pond to its source; the stream over there, that is blocked. Then, life-giving oxygen can resuscitate the remaining fish."

Everyone in the group is inspired to action like rescue-workers courageously moved to act by the chance of even finding one survivor. The work brings everyone together into a cohesive unit. They step out of the confines of their personal self to realize a connection, a nexus to something greater: to a cause full of benevolence. Even the hardness of Steven's heart, softens under the weight of suffering. He enjoys fishing but this seems a wasteful destruction to him.

A huge cedar log is blocking and diverting the stream that once brought life-giving water to the pond. Chandra ties two ropes around the logs and with the two groups united in resolve, they pull from two different ends until the log finally begins to budge. They have to put out more energy to get it completely dislodged. Even with more force, the log is difficult to move. Chandra joins the group along with Celeste, to give more weight to the effort. He directs the group, "Now on the count of three, everyone pull. Okay, one... two... three!"

Logan is the most motivated – he had been pulling the rope with all his strength. With a lot of effort, especially in that heat, this time the group acting in complete unison succeeds in removing the log and the stream begins to flow. Everyone spontaneously begins to cheer at that sight. In less than a minute, fresh water starts to flood the pond.

Experiencing the sight of death brings the group to affirming life, as they remove all the other debris that blocks the stream. Finally, the stream can be heard rushing into the pond. Its sound is so musical and delightful to their ears. Within an hour the health of the stagnant pond is restored. The fish that were gasping for air can now be seen swimming with vitality. The sight gives joy to the whole group; even Steven's harshness yields to a kindness that no one would have thought he possessed as he walks around with a big smile. He starts to remember himself in his younger years. An idealist to the core: He truly believed that he could change the world for the better. How bitterly disappointed he was when he realized that money makes the world go round and not love. Love is weak while money gives power. While he reflects, he feels Chandra's warm hand gently touching his shoulder.

"Compassion is the key to open your heart," Chandra whispers. "The place of greatest joy is in your heart."

The words pierce Steven's armour. For the first time, he starts to question the direction of his life. He realizes all his accomplishments were meaningless because he did not feel complete. Something was missing. What could it be, he wonders?

Logan approaches the two of them. He has a tear running down his cheek. He speaks with sadness: "You know, I've felt like crying for the past year but I couldn't. From the loss of my mother, my love, and even my self but today I could feel suffering that tore at my soul as I felt at one with the suffering of the dying fish. I could feel its energy waning away — its heart slowing and then stopping. When it died, it opened my heart to suffering outside my own pain. That fish exposed all the suffering I felt. I could no longer bear it but I had to release the tension through tears. You see that fish and this whole pond showed me that suffering exists all around us. The world is a very cruel place just like this pond."

For a moment silence fills the air. Then, Chandra clears his throat and speaks: "Logan, extreme suffering can be found in this world. When we see it or hear about it, we sometimes want to turn away. Often, we watch it passively as spectators like when we watch the news. But, when it touches our hearts, then we act. We act with compassion because we're moved. It's impossible to end all suffering, still we can reflect on it and realize that within suffering, the seed of compassion can be planted so long as we overcome our doubts, cynicism and inaction. You will find guidance within yourself. You'll do what's right if you attune to the small voice within you. We weren't able to save all the fish in this pond, nor can we eliminate suffering completely. Still, we can do our part."

"We can do our part," Steven mutters. "But, it won't make a great impact unless you are someone who matters: Someone powerful or influential."

"You're right, Steven. The circle of influence can vary. Some people may have influence over the globe like world leaders, celebrities, and even dictators with absolute power. Others may only have limited influence within their small communities, neighbourhoods, or families. Nevertheless, the impact of a person acting in a small way can be concentrated locally like the warmth of a campfire, instead of being diffuse like the sun's rays that envelop the earth. Both are needed for warmth, and so are valuable on their own merits. Influence can be exerted in far-flung areas by the rich and powerful but its effect is not felt at a deep level like a personal relationship, which touches your soul with love. One of the most important concepts to emerge from the environmental movement is to think globally but to act locally."

"Okay, you're kind of making sense," Steven admits with some reservation.

"Well, let's try something if you're willing," Chandra suggests.

Logan who had silently watched the discussion interjects: "I guess I'll also try it."

"Sure!" Chandra exclaims. "Would you please close your eyes? Imagine or visualize that you are a marvellous bird. Just see yourself as a great bird that soars higher, higher than the clouds. It doesn't matter the kind of bird: you can be an eagle, quetzal or even a condor."

A moment later, Chandra continues: "You have a panoramic view of the world but you realize that you cannot land. You can only view the world from a great distance. It gives you the ability to see far and wide but you cannot intimately touch or feel the world. You can only remain detached. This is how it is for someone powerful. They have a great vantage point though the details are missing. The heart can see a lot yet it intimately feels little. Now, when you are ready let go of the image, let go… when you are ready, nod your head."

When they nod their consent, Chandra continues: "Let yourself relax, allowing the images that I suggest to naturally come into your mind, without any effort. You have now turned into a serpent, a snake. It is of little consequence whether you are a cobra, rattler, viper or even a python. You crawl upon your ribs on the ground. Your vision is limited but you can taste the earth and particles in the air as they touch your forked tongue. You commune with everything around you in a physical, grounded manner. Being so intimately connected to existence, you cannot be removed from suffering or despair."

"This is like the person who dwells closely and intimately with life and even death. You are connected to suffering at an experiential level. It is not theoretical; rather it's all around you. Like suffering, you also experience other states such as joy, love, loneliness, inspiration and bliss. These are the elements that make up the fullness of life: Both in its delicacy and sharpness. We often want to encounter only positive feelings all the time and shrink from the negative ones. Isn't that so?"

His audience nods in consent. Then, he continues: "Open your eyes now. Okay. Do you see that stick on the ground?"

"Yes," Logan states curious where this is leading.

"Logan, please pick up the stick and hand it to me."

On receiving the stick, Chandra points to one side of it and says: "Think of this end of the stick as all the negative aspects of life like pain, suffering and loneliness; while the other end contains all the positive aspects like compassion, community and joy. The two ends are one and you cannot separate them. When you pick up the one end of the stick, you are accepting the other end of the stick."

After a brief pause, Chandra continues: "So, life also oscillates between the negative and positive. You cannot separate them, without destroying the indivisible whole. Divisions are created in the mind and not in reality, which always remains whole, undivided. That's why the Nexus of things surrounds us, while our mind veils this reality by its discursive thinking. Yet, the same mind that divides reality can also allow us to see its unity through inspiration, vision and intuition."

Another pause, and Chandra notes: "The wisdom of this wholeness is conveyed succinctly in the Taoist yin-yang, the Hindu symbol, the Sri Yantra with its multiple interlocking triangles emerging from the center-point. A Kabbalistic interpretation of the Star of David – also called the Seal of Solomon – suggests that it is a harmony of two principles like heaven and earth. The pentagram also represents wholeness with each point representing one of the five elements. The main point of all these symbols, except for the yin-yang, is the meeting-point at the center of two aspects. We are at the outer edges and our journey is to find the center. The yin-yang goes a step further in showing that polar opposites, rather than being exclusive, form the composite whole."

Logan argues: "That may be true but observing all the carnage in the pond, fills my mind with only images of death, destruction and despair. Where is the hope in this vision? It merely agitates my mind, reminding me of the immense cruelty of the world. Our earth is not a nice place: It is a place where suffering is not only tolerated but also boorishly celebrated in wars and environmental destruction. Hell is not in the hereafter; we are in it right now. If we remove our self-imposed blinders, we will realize that our existence is composed of one suffering after another. Life is miserable. All we can do is to tolerate it until we die." Then he adds in barely audible voice: "Or decide to exit."

Steven remarks: "Wow, Logan! Those are strong words. I don't know if I agree with you. I think money can make your life more comfortable; without it you will needlessly suffer. So, the source of happiness is to accumulate more and more wealth. Then, you can have happiness through security and comforts."

"Well, I haven't had any problem with money," Logan asserts. "My sadness arises from looking at the unbearable condition of the world. I can see the world realistically, while everyone else is hiding behind a fortress of positive thinking. Positive thinking doesn't change the world, no matter what visualizations or affirmations you use. Sorry if you're offended by my words, Chandra. But, it's the truth."

"Oh, no, I'm not offended," Chandra assures him. "What you are expressing is valid. You are merely looking at one end of the stick, which doesn't negate the other end. The world is a complex place: Full of wonders like the beauty of a flower, or beautiful sunsets, or sandy beaches, or the experience of love. On the other hand, the stark horrors of war, injustice and hate also exist in the same world. The world is not black and white as different levels of beauty, joy, and bliss can be experienced, as well as, co-existing degrees of pain, injustice, loneliness and despair. Don't you agree?"

"Well, not really," Logan counters. "I don't see much good in the world. Maybe, I'm seeing the glass half-empty but I seriously doubt it. I'm just more realistic in my appraisal than most people because I don't hide from bitter truths of life."

"You are observant, Logan. So, you will notice life in its aggregate parts. Since, you have experienced much suffering, your perception might be coloured. Interestingly, you said *much* of life is not good but even you admit goodness exists even if at a miniscule level. Isn't that so?"

"Well, maybe — um, what I mean is some goodness exists but it's so little that it doesn't make a difference. It doesn't remove the horrendous suffering and especially loneliness."

"Why especially loneliness?" asks Chandra.

"Because my experience right now is one of separation and isolation. No one can understand me. I feel like withdrawing from everyone, so that I can never be hurt again."

"Logan, love may hurt you. It may cut across your naked heart like a dagger. But, this vulnerability, this loss, makes you most human. Without it, how can you possibly understand another's suffering?"

"So?"

"So, instead of loss keeping you from reaching out to others due to fear of being hurt again, decide within your lonely heart's misery to reach out. Your pain unites you to all the suffering in this world, whether it is someone's grief, loss, loneliness, despair or hunger. Your own suffering is the source of expansion and when you reach out, you break the shell that imprisons your heart. You have to make the move. If you continue to wait: compassion, love, and even life will pass you by if you choose to stand on the sidelines wallowing in your own grief. It is a question of how you want to live your life: in fear or with courage. Which do you choose, Logan?" Chandra asks with a direct, penetrating look. His stare unnerves Logan for a moment; still he could see kind eyes waiting patiently behind the directness.

"Chandra, I have never heard you talk so frankly. I want to choose what's right. But, I don't know if I can. I don't want to be lonely but I don't know how to reach out. The compassion of my heart is encased in self-imposed armour."

"Then, I have a task for you. Tonight, as you go to sleep imagine or visualise a candle-flame melting the waxen armour around your heart. As it melts, remember all the suffering that you have gone through and how it has closed down your heart, until you see all the wax melt away, leaving behind the pure golden light of your compassionate heart."

"And?"

"At that point, consider love and compassion that resides at the center of your heart. Open up once again to that love, let all fear subside and no longer control you. Examine suffering, see it clearly, then let go, let go — realize its transitory nature and how with compassion, you can turn the suffering of your heart to the path by which you can relate to suffering of every being. Within suffering is the seed for overcoming loneliness, separation and isolation. Accept suffering, reflect on it, and then realize its universal nature. Think of your personal suffering. Do you believe that no one has experienced your suffering before? To each home comes death, separation and loneliness in due course. You are not alone. All of us experience them and by them we are united. The connection between us draws us to the centre, to the Nexus."

The words echo as they penetrate Logan's heart. He doesn't fully understand them but decides to try what Chandra taught because he is developing trust in him.

For the first time, Logan thinks of Chandra as a wise, old man. It comforts him to have trust in him. He feels a sense of humility and no longer wishes to argue with him in his stormy mind. Strangely enough, the turbulence of his mind becomes silent, as he desires only to learn.

As if sensing his state of mind, Chandra declares: "Logan, loneliness is your suffering right now. It is isolating you from the group. Due to it, you can't reach out to other group members, as you believe this condition is uniquely yours. But, I want to tell you: it isn't uniquely yours. All of us go through it. So, forget about others not understanding your plight. Someone will in time, don't stop giving people a chance."

"I'll try…"

"Most importantly, realize that the remedy for loneliness lies in having the courage to reach out. Put your hand out in friendship, in love and people will respond. By reaching out, you will create a community, which will overcome the loneliness experienced by all its members. Community and loneliness are polar opposites: One cannot exist in the presence of the other. Examine what kind of community will nourish your heart, mind and body. Then, create it by bringing in one person at a time. This retreat is a great place to start."

Logan absorbs the words and he resolves to give others a chance, yet Sarah hadn't given him a chance.

On the other hand, he hadn't thought of this retreat offering him a chance to create lasting friendships with others at the retreat: Steven, Muriel, Chandra and Celeste.

Logan realizes he's been too caught up in his emotional world with the unexpected appearance of Sarah at the retreat.

Chandra smiles: "Logan, tonight before you go to bed. I want you to read a beautiful poem by William Blake. I have left a copy of it under your door. Afterwards, imagine or visualize the armour around your heart like wax. Then, imagine a flame melting away the waxen armour. Hold onto this image as you fall asleep. Okay?"

Logan nods his consent, adding: "Thank you, Chandra, for your insights. I will do what you asked. In fact, I am tired. I think I'll retire early this evening," Logan adds as he yawns.

"I'm not tired," adds Steven. "Can I walk with you, Chandra, and ask you a few questions?"

"Sure, of course" Chandra replies.

"Well, I'm going to say good-night. Until tomorrow, my friends," Logan declares as he waves good-bye.

"Goodnight, Logan. Happy dreams," replies Chandra.
"Night, Logan," Steven also responds.

As Logan walks back to his cottage, he looks back at the two distant figures and feels positive about the retreat. After some reading, he would try the visualization that Chandra recommended. The fondness that he feels for his teacher makes him want to try out his instructions for himself.

Logan reflects on the experiences at the pond and Chandra's wise words. He considers: "Can it be that at the core of everything is a circle of unity that binds all life together?"

Can I see another's woe,
And not be in sorrow too?
Can I see another's grief,
And not seek for kind relief?
- Blake

7

Psychic Surgery

Logan finds a copy of Kahlil Gibran's book, *The Prophet,* and Blake's poem *On Another's Sorrow* at his cabin. He reads the poem feeling inspired with each line. Certain verses stand out and replay in his mind as he turns off the lamp beside him:

"Can I see another's woe,
And not be in sorrow too?
Can I see another's grief,
And not seek for kind relief?

Can I see a falling tear,
And not feel my sorrow's share?
Can a father see his child
Weep, nor be with sorrow filled?

Can a mother sit and hear
An infant groan, an infant fear?
No, no! never can it be!
Never, never can it be!

...Think not thou canst sigh a sigh,
And thy Maker is not by:
Think not thou canst weep a tear,
And thy Maker is not near."

As the words of the poem replay in his mind, they give him comfort and insight into words spoken earlier by Chandra. Logan realises that the heart is the portal to connect to one another. He feels great joy that sorrow or even loneliness is not an impediment to communication but rather is the doorway towards true understanding between people.

Logan realizes his error was to assume that no one could grasp the dimensions of his emotions. When in reality, everyone has endured this psychic burden at one time or another. As his mind becomes serene, he starts to drift off, but he remembers the visualisation.

He focuses his attention on his breath, and starts to breathe deeply into his diaphragm as explained by Chandra at a lecture on yogic breathing: the gist of which was to breathe into the belly not just the lungs.

As the breath becomes rhythmic, an image spontaneously comes to his mind. His heart is surrounded by thick metallic armour with barbs around it. He imagines his emotions as grey smoke underneath this armour — smoke that cannot escape as it is encased inside the armour. He senses the heavy weight of these emotions on his heart. He hears a female's voice imploring: "You are killing yourself! You will explode, if you don't release your feelings." It is Sarah's voice. Then, he remembers Chandra's suggestion.

Logan next visualises the armour turning from thick metal to soft wax, which feels less constricting on his heart. A red flame starts to burn the wax. It melts slowly bit by bit. In time it disappears with heavy emotional smoke being released into his body. With the release, he feels a shocking jab in his heart's centre as if stabbed by a knife. It reminds him of his panic attacks.

Whenever the panic attacks would occur, he would always wonder if this was the final one; whether his heart would beat so erratically that he would be left gasping for his final breath. Yet, this time he felt comfortable. He remembers to focus on his breathing and allow the tension to flow away. By doing so, panic does not grip him and he does not tense up his muscles or become constricted in his breathing.

As the wax disappears totally, another flood of images enters Logan's mind: His dying mother as he held her hand, Sarah slamming the door shut in his face. Then, his recalling his pain when he decided to take pills to kill himself. With each image, the pangs across his heart run like an electric current across water. It feels overwhelming but he hears Chandra persuading him to continue.

Logan persists. Suddenly, he beholds Sarah blowing a kiss to him. She adds: "I meant you no harm. Please forgive me!" He feels undeniable hurt, betrayal and abandonment. He loves her and hates her at the same time. The mere thought of her excites him but also reminds him of her betrayal.

He is drawn to Sarah like a honeybee to the alluring fragrance of a crimson flower. Yet, he wonders, will her petals of love gently engulf him with ambrosial passion, or trap him in their folds. He wants to embrace her but she is a mirage unable to quench his longing.

Holding her would be a delight but is it not like holding a rose with thorns? It will prick and draw blood while its fragrance is intoxicating. How can he ever forgive her, unless she admitted her fault? Without it, he would be without any armour. Only through this admission, could he hope to enjoy love's fragrance without being pricked by thorns of hurt.

Logan hears footsteps along with a heavy thump-thump sound. He asks: "Sarah? Is that you? What are you doing here?" He waits for a response but no one answers. He peers through his eyes but cannot see anything.

He is now surrounded by thick mist, reducing visibility to near zero. For a moment, he thought that he saw a woman's silhouette within the grey vapours. He calls out: "Who's there?" But, without receiving a reply, he decides that it was just his imagination. He closes his eyes feeling ready for sleep.

Once Logan closes his eyes, the sound of approaching footsteps and the thump of a metal object on the floor makes the hair on his neck stand up. He feels an eerie numbness throughout go up and down his spine. He wonders who or what it is but dares not to open his eyes. He hopes that this unexpected night intruder will decide to leave him alone.

Suddenly, he feels hot breath upon his neck. He imagines a ferocious bear above him ready to rip open his neck. Or, could it be a killer hiding out in the woods of the retreat? Maybe, his initial thought was correct. Could it be Sarah coming to him tonight, but why would she breathe so heavily like an animal?

Wavering between expectation and fear, he opens his eyes. He wants to scream but cannot. He wants to move but his body is frozen with dread. Above him stands a creature without a face: No mouth, no nose, no ears and not even eyes — just a blank, ghastly outline of a face. Could such a monstrosity be even said to have a face?

Logan surveys the rest of the creature. It is a female with large, full bosom and ten arms. In one hand, she carries a trident and in the opposite hand a dagger, which drips blood on his chest. Frightened, he manages to ask: "W-w-who are you?"

Deafening silence fills the room. Then, suddenly the creature attacks, striking Logan's chest with violent jabs. With a few slashing strikes, his chest is ripped open with a four-inch long incision revealing his fragile, beating heart. As she holds his heart with her many hands, her hands turn crystal and cool the heart, slowing it and then nearly stopping it. Then her dagger punctures his heart, and instead of blood oozing out grey smoke escapes from its chambers and fills the room. The vigorous stabs don't hurt Logan but release muscular tension, especially from his neck and shoulders. That tension was locked there from the time his despair began. He remembers when it first started: The day when he returned to California after losing Sarah, his shoulders became tight and painful. The pain extended upwards into his neck, and since then he carried this tension wherever he went.

The creature pauses. Logan realises this being reminds him of Hindu sculptures of goddesses and celestial maidens, though he couldn't identify which image. But, her many arms and trident make her appear like a deity. Her facelessness still frightens him like gazing into a mirror and seeing no reflection.

As he continues glancing at the "goddess," a large eye appears on her forehead at the third-eye point. It is a big Cyclops-like eye that emits golden light on his exposed, beating heart. The light warms and heals his heart. His heartbeat starts to quicken, and in time the warmth and relaxation spreads throughout his body.

Logan looks down at his chest and he realises his heart has been repaired. The "goddess" has restored his heart to vibrant health. He is filled with courage and joy, instead of negative, isolating emotions with this new heart.

He feels appreciative and just as he opens his mouth to thank her, she transforms into Sarah. Logan cannot believe his eyes. How did it happen? Was it Sarah all along? Before he can ask a question, she bends down and kisses him on the forehead, and whispers in his ear:

"Logan, I never meant to hurt you. I don't want you to suffer because of me; only you can heal yourself. It's up to you, my love. It's up to you…"

****

Darkness, darkness all around! What's going on? Logan hears his heart beating in total blackness.

He reaches out and after some fumbling turns on the lamp beside his bed.

His whole body and clothes are drenched in sweat.

He looks around to find Sarah or the "goddess," but he is alone. Besides the cadence of crickets outside, silence fills the air. He breathes a sigh of relief, with the realization that it must have been a dream.

The sound of the crickets gives way to the melodious songs of the first morning birds. He looks at his watch and realizes that the sun will be up within the hour.

Logan decides to go for a walk and to greet the first morning rays, as he doesn't dare to close his eyes, especially after a night full of strange visitations.

After the wonderful walk, Logan feels invigorated by the cool morning air and the sunrise gives him a feeling of renewal and strength.

Suddenly, Logan hears the sudden crack of a branch from the woods behind him. No one is there but he senses that someone is watching him. The woods are still dark even with the increasing sunlight and a mist seems to surround them. Remembering the night visitor, Logan decides to head for the open fields ahead and leave the dense tract of trees behind.

The sudden return of fear – from hearing a sound in the woods – makes him reconnect to the puzzling events of the previous night. He reflects on his experience. Was it all a dream?

If it was a dream, why does he feel changed and who is in the woods? Maybe, no one is there. He is just hearing things. Given his strange visions, he wonders if he is going crazy. Were the visions of last night just hallucinations?

Wondering, he opens the buttons of his shirt. He finds a four-inch long incision shaped like a sickle across his heart. The wound is certainly no dream. As he touches the tender flesh around it, Logan shudders with terror with the awareness that the night's events left a clear mark across his heart.

Filled with anxiety, Logan goes down on his hands and knees, and then lies upon the grass. His heart is racing and his body is drenched in sweat. This continues unabated for five minutes, until Logan remembers Chandra's advice to control his breathing when he feels anxious. After closing his eyes, he breathes deeply into his belly, envisioning blue, cool air going in and grey, toxic air being exhaled. Cool, blue air going in and dark grey air coming out. He repeats the process five times.

It works! He is able to control his panic attack with a few minutes of deep breathing and visualisation for the second time today. Logan feels comforted with the knowledge that he does have control.

His greatest fear was that he would die as his breakdown came full circle. Yet, now he feels safe with the knowledge that he can restore peacefulness with abdominal breathing.

The skill is deceptively simple but powerful, as Chandra had explained: "Breathing is something controlled by our subconscious that we ordinarily don't even notice. Nevertheless, emotions and breath are intimately interwoven. Whatever you feel affects your breathing and through your breath you can influence your emotional, mental and physical state. Tension or constriction in breathing creates mental tension. Tense thoughts create emotional tension, which is then stored within the body as tightness, knots and blockages in energy. Breathing deeply into your belly restores harmony and tranquillity, while shallow chest only breathing increases tension and negative emotions. Breathe into your belly, let it fill up with oxygen, and then fill up your lungs from the bottom up. You gasp for air when you're upset or in fear, but when you sleep soundly your breath is deep and rhythmic. Take a deep breath right now and restore health."

When Logan first heard these words, he felt like laughing because it seemed so deceptively simple. Now he realizes their deep significance. He resolves to pay attention to his breathing whenever he feels anxious.

Yet, as he reflects once again on the gash across his chest, he remembers the feature story he wrote on a female stigmatic. Her psychologist concluded that her emotions were so powerful that they created the suffering or passion of Christ on her body. Could his emotions have created the mark across his chest, or was it the work of a supernatural force?

A sudden rustle of branches makes him shudder. Logan might have the answer but he didn't want a repeat of last night. His breathing becomes restricted even with his training, as he imagines the faceless face of the goddess from the night. Should he run or prepare to fight? His body tenses for action. But, he dare not turn around and face the supernatural.

"Good morning, Logan!" booms Chandra's deep, resonating voice. Logan breathes a sigh of relief. His breathing returns to normal and his constricted muscles relax.

"Why are you out and about so early in the morning?" Chandra asks.

"Chandra," Logan smiles, "I'm sure glad it's you."

"Well, it sounds as if you weren't expecting me but perhaps someone else."

"Yes, I thought — well, it doesn't matter what I thought. Let's just say I had some intense dreams last night."

"Hmm, sounds interesting. Maybe, you'd like to share your experiences with me."

"Well, yes, but can we wait until later."

"Sure. Some yogis even say you can direct your dreams and even influence the dreaming of other people. In contemporary circles, it's called lucid dreaming. Don't forget to tell me about your dream as I always find dreams interesting. Dreams can be a window to the soul."

Logan considers if Chandra had influenced his dream that brought him to this retreat but he decides to remain quiet. Instead, he assures his teacher of his desire to share his dream: "Oh, I'll remember to fill you in on it," he says. Then he adds with a smile, "I can't forget it even if I try."

"I want to express the message to you that dreams often convey your inner emotional state. So, take them as markers but don't become frightened by them if they are intense."

"That's reassuring."

"Are you getting hungry, Logan?"

"To tell you the truth I'm famished."

"Well, how about if we cook something together. What would you like?"

"Oh, maybe a horse or two would do, even though I'm a vegetarian. But, after last night I need something substantial."

"I know just the thing," Chandra smiled. "It's a Punjabi recipe: little round balls made from linseed, butter and sugar called *pinnee*. We can wash them down with milk. How does that sound?"

"I guess it's good."

Chandra replies with a grin: "Trust me you'll like them. And, they're also good for you."

"I don't know if I'd like them if they're good for me. But, I trust your judgement, Chandra."

After enjoying a big breakfast including Chandra's recommendation, Logan feels contented. He reclines back in the easy chair in the large stone house and in that moment his mind is still, which is stillness based upon his mind enjoying the moment. Then, he hears a voice within. It says: "This too will pass."

And it does. His mind again becomes troubled as the appalling image of the faceless goddess surfaces. She stands with a trident in one arm, a sword in another, and finally the most grotesque sight – the back of a decapitated head – drips with blood in her other hand. She turns the head slowly around... it is Logan's.

Chandra clears his throat and rouses Logan from his macabre image. "You wanted to tell me about your dream. Do you want to discuss it now?"

After a moment's hesitation, Logan replies: "Why, yes. It's strange. I don't know where to begin."

"Start with what you recall first and then fill in the necessary details as they come to you."

Logan explains his nightmare to Chandra, who listens attentively. He hangs by every word and doesn't interrupt until Logan concludes: "Well, that's the peculiar vision from tonight. What do you think?"

"Just give me a moment. Let me collect my thoughts. Did you say that the deity figure turned into Sarah?"

"Yes."

"I believe that's the key to understanding your dream."

"How do you mean?"

"Just reflect on your relationship with Sarah. You two were once very close, true?"

"Yes, that's true."

"Do you feel she betrayed you?"

Logan feels like denying it but his feelings arise to the surface like pressured vapours that can no longer be contained. He vents: "Y-y-yes! Yes, it was like she plunged a knife in my back when she left me for Kurt!"

Chandra strokes his beard thoughtfully. "It's difficult what you've gone through, yet can't you see your feeling of betrayal and hurt makes you angry? It's anger that you've contained, but unless you can find a way of letting it go, it will slowly destroy you. This is what your dream is clearly communicating: The goddess figure is your twisted idol — an idol of the perfect woman mixed with betrayal and danger. She symbolizes that your perfect love in life, Sarah, fell from your ideals. Her love was fickle to you and so the "goddess" is faceless. She has no feelings, so how can she have a face? Then, let's look at what the goddess does next..."

"Well," Logan interjects, "she ripped open my chest."

"Exactly!" Chandra exclaims wisely. After noticing Logan's puzzled look, he goes on: "Let me explain: Your heart is the seat of emotions. So, when she rips open your heart it's like inflicting an emotional wound, though it doesn't stop there. After opening you up, instead of blood pouring forth, smoke surfaces. The smoke represents your inner emotional tension that you have stored away in your body from the mortal wound. If you recall: As the smoke escaped, the persistent tension left your neck and shoulders."

"Strangely, enough, that area still feels loose," Logan declares, as he rotates his neck in a circle.

"I'm not surprised. The dream and the events that transpired within the dream released you from emotions that were locked in your musculature. But, the next part of the dream hints at future possibilities. It hints at healing your emotional self. The rays from the third eye of the "goddess" are healing energy rays, which are accessible once you recondition your heart. Take away the hurt, the anger, the sorrow and replace it all with positive, healing emotions. Allow emotions to enter that open your heart up, instead of closing and constricting it from people in the world. Replace hurt, anger and bitterness with healing rays of love, compassion and acceptance. You can remove your isolation and loneliness by opening your heart. Would you like to try a visualisation exercise with me?"

"Maybe," Logan says hesitantly, "what's its purpose?"

"It helps you open up your heart and remove the emotional constrictions you have placed on it."

"Okay, let's try it. Do you want me to close my eyes?"

"Yes, that's right. Just relax in the easy chair and close your eyes. Allow your breathing to become nice and steady, without any effort — let it be natural. Relaxing deeper and deeper with each exhalation. Now, become aware of the beating of your heart. Count each beat in your mind until you reach ten. When you reach ten, raise your right index finger to let me know."

After receiving the signal from Logan, Chandra continues: "Now, that you know the rhythm of your heart, I want you to now slow down the count and match your heart rate with increasingly slower and slower counting of each number that I mention to you."

Chandra counts each number, starting with one and increases the space between each count until he reaches twenty. He continues: "Imagine your heart enclosed within hard waxen armour. Your heart is beating quietly under it. Underneath the wax are the petals of a lotus closed tightly. The wax surrounds the flower and it doesn't allow the petals to open. Imagine a warm light emanating from the lotus, which glows white under it. The warmth is healing. It releases negative, isolating emotions of anger, hurt, pain and sorrow. Allow these negative feelings to surface. They may be associated with events, thoughts or feelings. Let them arise and feel them fully. Bring them to the surface and feel them... now."

Logan suddenly feels a torrent of images flooding his mind and intense feelings associated with each. He remembers something — a memory he had forgotten or buried: John, his father, playing catch with him.

It was one of the few times John was sober for any length of time. John yelled to him: "Boy, don't you dare drop the ball!" When the ball glided through the air in slow motion, young Logan's mind froze.

Logan was petrified, afraid of disappointing his callous father. The ball fell to the ground with a thud like lead.

Everything speeded up, he remembers his father violently shaking him and hot tears running down the cheeks of the 12-year-old boy who only knew he was no good. Logan knew he was a disappointment to his father.

His father had harshly added: "Stop you're crying, you sissy! Be a real man, for God's sake!"

Logan remembers at that point clamping on his tears, burying them deep within. He was not a sissy and he understood he couldn't show his fear or disappointment ever again.

That day marked the beginning of Logan's suppression of his feelings.

Logan would never play catch with his father again because he would avoid John and John would avoid him. Logan took to books, a fantasy world where he could not be hurt or disappointed.

Hurt and rage surfaces as he thinks of his father now. *That man betrayed my mother and me.* With that thought, Logan clenches his fists and all the tension in his body goes to them, and then the tension dissipates. His fists loosen and drop. His whole body becomes limp.

Another memory surfaces: Standing outside Sarah's doorstep, cold and disappointed. She had left him. All the promises of eternal love were destroyed in an instant.

She betrayed him when he needed her most.

As he threw away the diamond engagement ring, he declared to himself that he would never allow himself to be hurt again. He would rather spend his life in loneliness, than to relive the hurt he felt at that moment.

The hurt surfaces as a knife jabbing his heart and he draws a fitful sigh.

Then, Logan recalls looking down at the casket, saying his last goodbye to his mother. He felt inexorable grief and sorrow as he saw her face radiant. The lines of tension and pain had left, yielding at last to death.

He felt completely alone then. Loneliness and hopelessness cast a shadow across his face. He faced his mother's loss alone.

His hope was that Sarah would be there with him at his mother's funeral. Sarah never attended the funeral.

From then on, Logan was certain no one could be trusted, especially when he really needed them. *People are around you for the good times and in difficulties they flee from you as if you were a ghost. So, it is better to smile on the outside, while you fall apart on the inside.*

Logan hears Chandra's words come into his awareness: "... light melts away the waxen walls. The insidious emotions of sorrow, hurt and anger soften away under the white light. Now, the wax has completely dissolved. The lotus opens its petals like your heart opening up to the world with love. Bitterness has no place in your heart, which is now filled with a golden light of love. Bask in this light."

Chandra pauses, then continues: "Allow your heart to be fully open and lose all fear of being hurt. Your hurt is not an isolated event; it is the fabric of human experience from which mystics, poets and writers have gained insight. Opening the heart emotionally like the flower opening its petals is the first step to reclaiming your connection to being fully human. As your heart petals open fully, you will through empathy reconnect to the human family. Your suffering brings full understanding and empathy of each hurting heart. When you heal and understand your suffering, you can heal the brokenness of another heart."

Logan takes a deep breath. He exhales and feels all the emotional tension stored in his body leave.

Chandra continues: "Replace hurt and fear with an awareness that your suffering is not separate. It does not isolate you from humanity or other creatures, rather through your suffering you become most connected — most in touch with everyone around you. Your own heart's loneliness leads you to connect with others, for who among us at some point in our lives has not suffered from pain, loneliness, disappointment."

Logan quietly nods agreement, as Chandra adds: "Isolation as a means to avoid hurt, pain or any other unsettling emotions is futile just as you cannot hide from the brilliance of the sun or the darkness of a still night. So, face the disturbing affliction squarely and turn it into a necessary condition for enfoldment. Allow the heart's lotus to blossom and replace the prison of wax that isolates it. As the lotus opens its petals, heal the hurt you have carried within you. Begin the slow process of forgiving, of letting go of past hurt. Let it go, slowly, slowly... whenever you are ready... you can do it, now or later. Will you, Logan, try to forgive past transgressions?"

Logan nods in consent.

"Great! First, forgive yourself," Chandra instructs.

In confusion, Logan's brow furrows. Even though, he feels deeply relaxed, he asks: "What do you mean forgive myself?"

"Well," Chandra explains, "you must forgive yourself for not allowing yourself to feel. You buried the hurt and pain way down inside. You did not allow it to come up, except in a moment of anger and especially as virulent despair, which became your only expression of inner dread. The uneasiness, rooted in feelings of loneliness and isolation, gave way to anxiety, melancholy and hopelessness."

"That's very true," Logan says softly.

Chandra smiles, then elaborates: "You have learned, here at this retreat, to cope with anxiety through breathing and relaxation techniques. Now, your melancholy can only be assuaged through uncovering its roots, namely, repressed emotions…"

Logan sighs with the realization that the words Chandra speaks are true and speak directly to his soul.

"Ask yourself in a quiet setting," Chandra continues, "what is really troubling me? Is it your emotional baggage that you carry? What emotions are present behind the feelings of sadness?"

As silence fills the air, Logan starts wrestling with these questions. He uncovers nothing, at first, but then: The vivid re-enactment of the door slamming in his face, as he stood outside in the cold snow, surfaces.

He hears the sound repeat and repeat in his mind until it reverberates.

Then, a voice, his voice, whispers: "You feel hurt and have closed down to love. You remain isolated out of fear. You have locked your heart and thrown away the key." Logan imagines a big keyhole in the centre of his heart without a key to unlock it. He mutters out loud, "I need to find the key to unlock my heart."

"What key will unlock your heart?" Chandra asks.

At first, Logan consciously can't think of what this key could be. Then, he allows his subconscious mind to guide him. After a few minutes, Logan responds: "The key that opens up my heart is to dare to love again, without fear of being hurt."

"Very good!" Chandra confirms. "Then, see this key opening your heart, now… What transpires?"

"The key now opens my heart. I realise it isn't a physical key. It is something within me. I have locked my heart and I can also unlock it."

"How?"

"Well, my heart was unlocked in that moment when I felt at one with the dying fish in the pond. Somehow observing his suffering made me recognize that my suffering and his torment were one. I couldn't be isolated, locked in the prison of my heart, when I reached out to the fish in compassion and with total empathy, felt its sorrow as intimately as my own. As I opened up my heart, it made me understand I can love again. Tenderness of the heart was not alien to me as I forced myself to believe. Compassion, love and kindness can unlock the heart."

"You have solved the question, Logan!" Chandra exclaims as he squeezes Logan's hand.

Logan regains full conscious awareness. He feels healed as if his fragmented heart is put back together again.

His heart feels unrestrained and he feels like dancing with the wind and walking freely with friends and companions.

Logan's heart had been put under a frightening psychic knife. Yet that knife started the process of unlocking his emotions. A process that had only just started and wasn't fully complete.

Isolation as a means to avoid hurt, pain or any other unsettling emotions is futile just as you cannot hide from the brilliance of the sun or the darkness of a still night. So, face the disturbing affliction squarely...
- Chandra Singh

8

Revelations

Celeste is elated as she watches Logan from a distance. "Logan really seems to have changed. He came out of his protective shell. It's amazing!" she exclaims.

"Yes, I'm telling you he's headed in the right direction," Chandra replies while stroking his beard thoughtfully and observing Logan's distant silhouette in the twilight. Chandra can also make out a second silhouette – Logan has a companion.

While Celeste and Chandra continue conversing outside the old stone building, Logan is enjoying an evening stroll near the woods with Muriel.

Unnoticed by either of them, Steven has been steadily walking briskly towards them, coming up from behind in hopes of joining the conversation. And he's now within hearing distance.

Muriel looks over at Logan and turns to him.

"Logan, you're right about being frank and open. I've wanted to share something with everyone at this retreat. But, I didn't want to trouble people with my problems. Aside from Chandra and Celeste, no one knows," Muriel confides.

"I don't think you should feel you have to hold back," Logan assures her. "You can feel comfortable with everyone at the retreat. We have a caring, spiritual community here. You have nothing to hide."

"That's wonderful!" Muriel smiles. "You don't know how musical your words are to my ears. I have wanted the comfort of a spiritual community before I go."

"Go? Where are you planning on going so late?" asks Steven, a little out of breath from trying to catch up to them.

"I will tell you in a moment. Could you ask Celeste to come over here?" Muriel asks.

"Sure," Steven replies. He returns moments later with a puzzled looking Celeste.

"What is it, Muriel? Is everything okay?" Celeste asks.

"Oh, everything's fine," Muriel confirms. "But, I want to tell them, now."

"Are you sure?"

"Yes, it's the right time."

The group walks closer to the building and the others are quickly rounded up. Celeste calls everyone's attention as they gather around Muriel, who stares far away into the horizon.

The setting sun has set the sky ablaze in reds and oranges. *Isn't it odd that the last rays of the day would be so brilliant,* Muriel ponders. She then clears her throat. She wonders where to start but she slowly begins: "I came to this retreat, seeking a place of rest. As I knew our teachers, I knew it was the right place for me as my final resting-place, a place of comfort in my pain."

Muriel hesitates for a moment, observing her audience. Then, she continues after being reassured by the kind expression on their faces: "The doctors have told me I have only a few months to live. So, I wanted my last moments to be in a beautiful place surrounded by love. My dream all of my life, especially after Pierre's death, was to find a community where I could belong. I have found it here with all of you."

She again pauses for a moment, as a smile lights up her face. Then she continues: "Even with the admirable display of yoga by Logan and Steven during the first class, we have created a spiritual center at this retreat. This gives me great joy to have spent what might be my last moments surrounded with the beauty of the countryside and wonderful people, instead of sterile hospitals. A loving environment can do wonders for the spirit."

Muriel gazes briefly at her friends gathered around her in a semi-circle. "Now, I don't want you to feel sorry for me. I want you to disregard the fact I am sick and won't live long. I'm alive and I'll savour each moment – and that is what I want you to do."

Even with Muriel's admonition, no one can help but feel dejected. Stillness fills the air like the silence at a funeral, as if mourning had already started.

The quiescence is disturbed by a strong gust, which blows a solitary leaf from a tree as the last rays of the day expire. The break from the branch is sudden and swift. But, it was inevitable. The leaf had a historical time-span that came to an end with the force of the agent of death, the wind, tugging at her tiny lifeline to the branch.

The leaf floats and dances with the breeze, as if still alive. Then, after hovering for a moment, it gently falls upon Muriel's lap. She has a tear in her eyes, and with a sad voice testifies: "This leaf had an unseasonable death. Fall was its rightful time to break from the branch but the forces of nature sealed its fate."

Tears well up in Muriel's eyes as she continues: "Death is inevitable and when you're old you want to leave to meet departed loved ones. But, you're afraid. I don't think I'm ready. How do you ever prepare?"

Steven clears his throat and states: "You know, great medical advances are possible. They cost money but..." Steven hesitates while he looks intently at Muriel. Compassion wells up inside of him, as he gazes upon the old woman's gentle face. He continues in a slightly wavering voice: "...if you need help with a new treatment, I'm willing to help you. I can pay for it."

Sarah wasn't as surprised by Muriel's sad news, as by Steven's gesture of kindness. Muriel had confided to her about being ill – though she had stopped short of saying the illness was terminal – and she witnessed the older woman's delight after the herb that Logan retrieved had eased her pain. Now, Steven had always made it clear money was all that mattered to him. Had she misjudged Steven? Was there more to him beneath his arrogant remarks?

"Oh, Steven, that is really kind of you," Muriel smiled, "but I know that the doctors have tried everything. I have to accept whatever fate has in store with courage."

With Muriel's news, a sense of fellowship is palpable within the group. Sometimes tragic news can unite people, since circumstances seem more defined. The egoistic frame of reference yields to something greater: A realization that life is not merely about what I can get, it is at its core a journey of letting go — ultimately, even letting go of life itself. Even Steven's hubris softens before the awareness that money can't protect you against death. However, after coming out of his self-imposed emotional confinement, Logan is especially troubled by the news.

At first, Logan is startled by Muriel's revelation. He feels a connection with her for her kindness. The news troubles him even with his expanded awareness, new beliefs and compassion. It reminds him of all his past loses: His disappointment at an absent dad, his mother's death, losing Sarah, and loss of own self in suicidal thoughts. His eyes become watery.

Sensing his sadness, Sarah walks towards him and touches him on the shoulder, and consoles him with words whispered in his ear: "Don't despair, Logan. As Muriel said let's make each moment beautiful. Life is too short for regrets. Wouldn't you agree?"

Logan nods but isn't sure what she means. He wants to push her away because he remembers his hurt but he also wants to be comforted, so he holds his hand out for her. She takes it and gently squeezes it. Even in despair, her touch excites Logan's heart. He starts to feel guilty for being happy in this sad moment but realizes his concern is unfounded once he observes Muriel.

She saw them reaching out to one another, and now she smiles, reassuring him she is not displeased. In fact, she is delighted, since she understands Logan's suffering at being separated from Sarah.

Muriel next announces to the group: "I don't want my words to make you despondent. I want to be surrounded by joy, love and good things of life. I'm alive now that's what matters. Let me share happy moments with you. If you change your attitude or treat me differently, then I will be unhappy that I told you anything. So, make an old woman happy through our closeness and *joie de vivre*."

After a moment's hesitation, she continues: "But, before I can enjoy anything, I need to rest. I guess my disclosure today took a lot out of me."

Sarah asks: "Do you want me to stay with you?"

"Oh no, dear," Muriel replies, "I can manage on my own. After a good night's rest, I'm sure I'll be fine tomorrow."

Chandra responds, "Celeste and I can accompany you to your cottage. We're headed that way ourselves."

"Oh, that would be nice. It'll give us a chance to talk."

The three figures head out into the night after saying farewell to everyone else. In her hand, Muriel keeps the fallen leaf. She has decided to keep it as a reminder of life's brevity.

Unlike the leaf, she knows the time of her break and has consciously decided to complete the rest of her days surrounded by nature, spiritual people and inspiring words. Her faith assures her the end was not with physical death but she was terribly afraid of dying alone in a sterile environment. Yet with her companions at the retreat and nature's beauty, she feels a sense of joy. Moreover, the image that she would happily join Pierre in heaven gave her great hope.

"She is such a nice woman," Steven comments. Then, he adds speaking as if he were asking himself, "Why is it the good ones that always seem to suffer?"

"What do you mean?" Logan asks puzzled.

"Oh, nothing!" Steven responds in an irritated tone.

"Don't take it personally, Steven – he's just asking," Sarah objects. "You don't need to get upset."

"Yes, you're right," Steven concedes. "It's just that Muriel is a nice woman and what's happening with her reminds me of a good friend that I knew. We were really close with big dreams about making it big as musicians."

"Musicians?"

"That's right, Sarah. I'm not really as shallow as you think I am. I became this way for a reason."

"What reason?" Sarah presses, suddenly curious.

Steven now looks alarmed. "I can't... I won't... I don't want to discuss it any further. Good night!" he yells as he briskly walks away into the night.

"What was that all about?" Sarah asks, puzzled.

"I'm not sure. But, it makes me certain that Steven has a complex history, which would surprise us. And, underneath everything, he does care."

"Yeah, I think so too."

"Well, Sarah, it's getting late. Shall we say good-night?"

"No, wait Logan. I — I don't want you to leave me. I don't want to be alone tonight. Hearing Muriel's news, I realize that life is too short and missed opportunities may never come back."

"What? What do you mean?"

"I want you to be with me, tonight."

"I don't understand," Logan replies feeling perplexed. He was just getting over Muriel's announcement and couldn't process Sarah's words. At that moment, he feels both attraction and anger towards her. He still loves her but he remembers the hurt and pain she caused him. How could he forgive her? Yet, without forgiving her, could he move on with his life?

"Logan, life hasn't been kind to either of us. I want to tell you..." Sarah trails off, hesitating.

Logan encourages her: "Go on. Tell me what?"

"I can't — not right now."

"If you're playing games with me, Sarah, I'm leaving!"

Sarah takes hold of Logan's arm as he turns his back on her to walk away. "No, I'm not being insincere with you. I only want what's for the highest good."

"Highest good? That pain that you caused me and your coldness were they also for the highest good?"

"I'm *so* sorry you're hurt. It wasn't my intention."

"I don't care about your intentions. I only know the results of your actions. Do you believe in karma, Sarah?"

"I suppose I do."

"Well, just remember my hurt will come back to you three-fold," Logan scornfully adds with his intense eyes glaring accusingly at Sarah.

She breaks down and now sits on the grass with tears running down her cheeks, and then fitful sobs. Finally, she loses control and weeps loudly. Logan is surprised and his anger quickly subsides. He reaches out to her, putting his hand on her shoulder.

"I'm sorry," he whispers. "I didn't mean what I said. My words came out sharp but I don't want you to cry."

Logan pauses, noticing that Sarah regains composure. She asks in a wavering voice: "I need you to hold me... make my nightmare end..."

He wants to ask her what she meant but decides just to tightly embrace her, allowing her to place her head on his shoulders while consoling her with his secure embrace. With that warm hug, tender affections envelop their hearts. Anger and insult give way to compassion and consideration.

Logan asks: "Are you feeling better?"

"Yes, somewhat better. Thank you."

"No need to thank me." As he hears the sound of an owl somewhere, he adds: "Now, take my hand and I'll walk with you to your cabin."

They walk hand-in-hand and Sarah feels so safe having Logan beside her for protection. She wonders if she is doing the right thing, allowing herself to get close to him. She isn't safe to be around. If Logan gets close to her, she could put him in danger.

Suddenly, Sarah remembers Kurt playing with a gun and pointing it at her with a wry smile. His words terrify her as she remembers them. He avows menacingly: "If you leave me, I promise you that I will kill you! And I'll kill any bastard I catch with you!" He then put away the gun and asked: "But you're not planning on leaving me are you?" Not waiting for an answer, he continues: "You can never leave me. Wherever you go, I will track you down because I love you. I will never let you go!"

Sarah's horrible thoughts are interrupted with Logan announcing: "Well, here we are."

They stand outside the cabin and decide, though no words are spoken, to wait a while and drink in the cool night air before going inside the cottage abode.

The cabin seems so dangerously placed to Sarah, enveloped in dark, mysterious shadows.

With Logan beside her, those shadows after a long time had briefly retreated.

Now, with the prospect that Logan would leave, she feels vulnerable again.

"Logan, thank you for bringing me safely back to my cabin. Often, I would help Muriel during the night, not only for her sake but also mine. But, this evening she needed time alone. I'm afraid of being by myself. Please keep me company tonight."

"Sure," Logan replies, "it'll give me an opportunity to make up for my outburst earlier."

"I really appreciate it, Logan. More than you can know."

As the moonlight envelops Sarah, for the first time that evening Logan notices how beautiful she looks.

With confidence in his words, Logan declares: "I just wanted to tell you that I think you're…"

He pauses for about four seconds, allowing the drama of the pause to take effect, and then finally confesses, "…beautiful."

Sarah smiles, adding: "Thank you for noticing. You mean it just dawned on you now."

"Don't be silly. I've always known your beauty. I just had no opportunity to say it before."

"I guess I should return your compliment. You also look beautiful."

"Hmm: Calling a man 'beautiful' I wonder if that's a good thing…"

"Well let me rephrase: You look absolutely handsome and debonair. Is that better?"

"Why, yes."

Sarah smiles, pleased that Logan likes her compliment, as she loved being told she's beautiful. She hadn't heard a nice compliment for so long. Oh how she had missed Logan.

They both reminisce of times they shared together.

The memory is bittersweet, as it is a moment regrettably past, lost in the abyss of wounds, hurts, and the gap of distrust that separates two hearts once united.

Yet, somehow it is soothing like remembering a time of

innocence and love: Of first love without the shadow of loss and sorrow.

"Are you remembering the past like me, Logan?"

Logan doesn't reply but nods in agreement and then he smiles. A passing thought came to him, which he did not want to share with Sarah.

The crisp night air feels exhilarating at that moment to Logan, broken only by the hooting of a far away owl and the sound of crickets. All sounds seem musical now because he has resolved everything in his mind. His body had ached to be with Sarah but he denied his passions.

Logan didn't know how she would respond. But, he would let the night run its course, without inhibitions. With that decision, he feels uplifted, filled with desire and longing for love. His longing would find stillness in thoughts of each touch, which would be an expression of uninhibited passion.

All the strange dreams beginning with the precognition of Chandra in a fantasy and most recently the strange visit by the "goddess," make Logan confused as the veil between reality and imagination is removed. He wonders if Sarah or even her cabin is real. *Am I dreaming this whole scene?*

As if in response to his thought, Sarah takes hold of his hand and smiles — the smile that Logan always loved. She has to be real when her hand is warm and her smile is as sweet as he remembered. He intertwines his fingers with hers and gently squeezes.

Sarah reciprocates his squeeze. They smile and tenderly kiss. Their warm lips touch and that moment is eternal, as time itself stops for the two lovers for whom the present moment only remains. For Logan and Sarah the pleasure of their lips pressing tightly together is breathtaking.

Even in the cool night air Logan's body is fervent with passion. His longing, desire is focused on his true love. He is no longer fixated with problems but regains his old self-confident air. Sarah always admired his certitude. Around him she always felt completely comforted. These feelings return like waves of delightful excitement.

Sarah truly needs to be comforted and Logan's presence

makes her feel protected. Her safety and the safety of others at the retreat weighed on her mind but all her worries, at least for tonight, could be forsaken.

As they enter Sarah's cottage, they notice the cool night air and the beauty of the sky. The full moon hangs in the starry sky, emitting its magical light on this enchanted night, which gives the nightscape a fantastic luminescence. Even the trees seem to glisten and shimmer in dancing moonbeams as if they are lightly sprinkled on this warm summer night with frost. They enter Sarah's room, which is dark as soft moonlight glistens through the window.

An air of romance, sensual delight, and desire fills the room. The two bodies glistening in the moonbeams hold hands, embrace and potently kiss. It's a kiss that makes the soul quiver with joy and expectation. Their hearts beat as one in unison to their soul's deepest yearnings. Logan wants this delightful moment to last forever.

Finally, he has his love. Sarah's figure stands naked before him and her curvaceous body glistens in the moonlight like an ethereal angel, or an exquisite porcelain doll.

A warm touch melts the skin's defences with gentle caresses arousing the inner fire of passion, desire and lust. Logan relaxes fully, allowing pleasure to build, as Sarah strokes and kisses him. All the tension resulting from self-denial dissolves with each touch. He gives in to his passions and yields fully to each touch.

She pushes him down firmly onto the bed, whispering in his ear: "I want you, Logan!" Then, she adds with a playful grin: "But I promise to be gentle."

Logan lies back. This special night and its sensual pleasures would be something both lovers would never forget. They experience ecstatic waves of sensual pleasures.

When it reaches a crescendo, Logan experiences something he never experienced before. With a sudden rush of energy, a luminescence surrounds both lovers. In that instant, he feels his ego and its defences melting away, as the lovemaking reaches a climax. It is an exhilarating moment where energy transforms the physical into the spiritual.

One can decide either to yield to the moment, or remain disconnected from true experience of union by your ego defences. Logan at one level wants to let go, yet fear of being hurt again holds him back. So he stays in the emotional shell created by his ego. The moment of ego-transcendence passes and Logan remains constricted in his heart, unable to merge.

Sarah, on the other hand, has no fears. Her fears become remote, as she feels safe and secure with Logan. It is a comfort that had remained remote and inaccessible to her for so long. All her problems melted away with physical and emotional closeness to Logan. Her ego yields to the moment to a feeling akin to rapture. She feels comforted, whole and centered. Instead of being self-involved, her awareness extends outwards and she clearly understands Logan's pain, which is intimately connected to her own. She resolves to tell him everything. But, right now she just wants the warm, intense feelings to enfold her being.

Sarah determines that when they wake up tomorrow, she will share her affliction with Logan. With that thought, she smiles and drifts off peacefully into a restful sleep.

****

The morning sun dances, breaking through trees swaying gently outside Sarah's window. She feels content after spending the night with Logan. Kurt seemed a distant memory when she was in Logan's secure arms. As these warm images comfort her mind, she keeps her eyes closed. Then, she has a desire to greet her lover with a warm embrace. She stretches her arm out to touch Logan. But, he isn't there.

Sarah opens her eyes, somewhat bewildered. Why would he get up so early and slip away so quietly? She then smiles. *Sweet Logan,* she thinks, *you didn't want to disturb my sleep. But, I don't care for sleep when I can see your wonderful face to greet the new day.*

As Sarah lingers in the bed, she remembers the beautiful

night she spent with Logan. It was an exquisite, enchanted night, which allowed her to reconnect with her buried desires. Whatever the future may hold, she is certain of her love for him. Her fears seem so very far away as if she is now released from them. *Where is my wonderful Logan?* she wonders.

Sarah decides to search for him. The early morning is beautiful with invigorating rays of the sun and cooled with a gentle breeze in which wildflowers gently sway in the field before her. To Sarah the colours today seem brighter and the sights and smells are more intense than usual. She feels free like a bird released from a cage. Sarah reflects: *What a wonderful moment to be in love again and to be surrounded by nature's beauty.*

Two chipmunks chase each other around the trunk of a big oak tree. Birds chirp in sweet voices and the Cardinal's bright red plumage can be seen as it flies from the oak to a maple tree. Even the distant cawing of a crow seems melodious to Sarah, for she is in love. And, in true love the senses are reformed, since perception discerns a newness in experience and elevates the ordinary into extraordinary. It imbues upon all senses a new awareness through which the world is envisioned full of laughter, joy and beating of the heart. The universe seems to dance to an inner melody that only the individual lover perceives in the heart.

Impersonal experience becomes intimately personal, and so poets write verses that penetrate the soul, and move the heart and senses. All these sensibilities make Sarah want to cling to the object of her passion.

She is now walking outside Logan's cabin and her heart tells her he is inside sleeping like a lamb. Her heart cannot wait. She must declare her love to him this instant. Sleep can wait but her love can no longer be patient.

So, she opens the cabin's door, which creaks rather loudly. As her eyes adjust to the room's dim light, she observes Logan sleeping in his bed. His body is tangled in the bed-sheets and his forehead drips with perspiration. Sarah quietly slips beside him and whispers in his ear: "Good morning, Logan."

She waits for a response and then adds in a barely audible voice: "I love you, my dear."

Logan stirs, suddenly opening his eyes, asking: "W-w-what are you doing here?"

"I decided to surprise you."

"Surprise me? Why?"

"Well, we had a great night and I wanted to see you. Why did you slip away without telling me?"

"Look, Sarah," Logan snaps, "let's forget about last night."

"What?" Sarah asks perplexed.

"Yesterday shouldn't have happened. It was a mistake."

"I don't understand. I believe it was a beautiful night like a real dream."

"Well, maybe for you. For me it was more like a nightmare," Logan scornfully adds.

"How can you call something so magical a nightmare?"

"Look Sarah I am tired of you and your games. So, I want you to leave and don't come near me again."

"You don't mean that."

"I sure do!" Logan yells, while holding the cabin door open and motioning Sarah to exit.

He adds with bitterness: "Leave, right now!"

Sarah is completely bewildered as she stands outside Logan's cabin with the door slamming behind her. The birds, the flowers, even the chipmunks, which during her last walk delighted her, now seem to tease Sarah with their happiness.

A tear trickles down her cheek as she remembers the day Logan came to her that cold evening. When he came back after his long absence and his mother's loss, and she closed the door upon his face. He too must have felt this ache that she now feels. She mutters as she walks back dejected to her cabin: "I'm so sorry, Logan, for causing you pain that day."

Does this path have heart? If it does, the path is good; if it doesn't, it is of no use. Both paths lead nowhere; but one has a heart, the other doesn't. One makes for a joyful journey; as long as you follow it, you are one with it. The other will make you curse your life. One makes you strong; the other weakens you.
-Carlos Castaneda, *The Teachings of Don Juan*

9

The Nexus Connection

A solitary silhouette, bronzed by the golden blaze of the mid-day sun is alone, with the fires of her soul pouring forth their heated cries. Sarah, of compassionate spirit, knows the heights of joy and the depths of sorrow that only sincere, selfless kindness bestows upon her.

Yes, she has known her share of suffering and yet it only serves to strengthen her, to rise above any personal pain or insecurity in order to be there as loving kindness personified for anyone in need.

Yet this particular high noon finds her on her knees with hands folded gently together in a heart-felt prayer, she whispers: "Dear Eternal One, please hear my prayer. I have been looking for Muriel for hours and she is nowhere to be found. Is she somewhere in the fields dying alone? Or is she lost, having wandered off too far? Guide me to her. Her health is failing. I must find her in case she is in need of help or comfort. Help me, guide me, please."

Given the fear that Kurt invoked in her, Sarah had turned more to prayer than ever. In her life, she had always found inner guidance. Her conscience was almost always clear on what direction to take but the threat of Kurt's violence kept her from making the break from him. Sarah recalls the first time Kurt became enraged. She had gone shopping, and she had met Dorothy, her best friend from High School. They had a lot of catching up to do, so they decided to go for coffee. When she came home she found Kurt tearing through her dresser. She thought that he had lost something.

"What are you looking for, Kurt?" she asked with concern.

"You're not the one asking questions here. I am!" Then, he grabbed her shoulders and pinned her to the wall.

"Where were you, Sarah? And you better not lie to me! Or else…"

"I'm sorry I just met a friend and we went for coffee."

"That's not good enough! I come home after a hard day and find you gone. Were you thinking of leaving me? You'd better not be. Because I love you so much that I won't let you leave."

Then he kissed her. She was at a total loss with his behaviour. As his jealousy increased, she realized that she was becoming trapped, isolated with Kurt having power and control over her. He would not let her go out alone. Whenever she did go out he would often follow her and start accusing her of having an affair, or planning to leave him.

She remembers another time when he violently flew into a rage. She didn't have dinner ready for him when he came home. So he demanded that she drop everything else and make his dinner. Sarah felt more and more like a slave to a bully instead of being in a secure, loving relationship.

When she had brought out the hurriedly prepared meal, he screamed: "What's this? You call this food? I wouldn't even feed this shit to a dog?"

Then, the vein in his temple throbbed and his face became white. He threw the plate across the room; barely missing Sarah's shocked face. The plate hit the wall, smashing into tiny pieces, which she later had to clean up. While Kurt apologized after a few days, his violence always re-emerged, sometimes cold and calculated at other times frighteningly furious.

Now at the retreat, Sarah was trying to reconnect to her intuition, to her ability to find guidance. She knew she had to make a decision but with all the abuse she suffered, Kurt had placed her in a submissive, powerless role and if she spoke, she would face his anger. She used to be able to speak her mind but now fear made her passive.

Even with ongoing abuse, Sarah for the longest time hoped that he would somehow change and when he appeared to be sincerely sorry after every explosion, she believed him. Yet each time she was disappointed when the cycle of violence would repeat itself in a predictable manner. In time, she was conflicted between emotions of love and hate for him, since her experience went from wonderful to dangerous.

She had now determined to leave him but she feared his retaliation. How he would strike out, she didn't know. But given his behaviour, she was terrified of a violent outcome. She didn't worry about her safety but for the safety of everyone at the retreat.

Given Kurt's insane jealousy, she is most concerned about what he might do to Logan. While she wants Logan, she is glad in a way that he pushed her away because it's probably the best for his safety to be far from her.

She had allowed herself joy with Logan, yet she never intended to place him in danger. So, she learned to accept her separation from him as being for the highest good, though her heart is torn apart. She wants to protect everyone else no matter what happens to her. Somehow she would deal with Kurt but she shuddered at the thought of being near him. She needed to escape from him, or die in the attempt.

I don't know what to do about Kurt. He's immobilized me with fear like a hunted animal. And I hate what he's done to me! I hate it! Sarah cries in her mind.

Then she declares to herself: *He goes on the back burner for now and I trust with more time at this retreat that everything will become clear. This retreat gives me the space I need and I've experienced great joy with Logan.* Suddenly she remembers Muriel: *Right now I need to focus. Where could Muriel be?*

Sarah slowly stands up and quietly spins around in a circle with her eyes closed in an attempt to sense the best direction that her next steps would take.

"This is it, yes this feels right" she softly speaks, as she looks toward the stream in the distance. Since she came to the retreat, she had been struggling to regain her confidence in her capacity to make decisions. She wanted to trust her actions, without the nagging doubts and fears that Kurt had implanted in her mind over the past year. Being under his control had made her lose touch with her strength. Now at the retreat she is regaining her confidence.

Sarah is wise beyond her years. At the young age of twenty-five she has trust in prayer, and knows how to listen to her body for guidance. If she hadn't met Kurt, she would not have lost her sense of direction. In the past, her intuition had worked for her, so she never felt lost, unlike her friends who struggled with choices. Now she was petrified by fear.

With her blue eyes sparkling, the earth feels solid and secure beneath her feet as Sarah earnestly begins her search. As her hair glistens Sarah knows that if she had the environment to live like this she would peacefully live out her intuitions by following higher guidance.

Yes that's it, I need to start listening to my body again, to my heart's deepest feelings, my higher guidance, and then I'll know my way, without any fear for what might happen.

Finally Sarah stands beside the stream in awe. *How beautiful.*

A profusion of red flower petals drift playfully along the surface of the waters; then more and more petals. Sarah cups some of these petals into her hands and then watches them drop to the water. She looks at her hand and it reminds her of the shape of a heart and a human figure at the same time. In that instant, she realizes something about the whole retreat.

Nexus involves heart-centered living and allowing your heart to freely open and blossom. These petals in her hands represent that progression from a closed bud to an open flower. The open flower has the scent of love-nectar, which attracts bees and other insects to it. Without opening of the petals, the male pollen would not be carried by the wind or insects to the female parts of the plant in order to fertilize the plant. Similarly, if the human heart remains closed, then a person will remain isolated but once the petals of the heart open then connection and relatedness is established. Through empathy and compassion, the heart can reach out to others. The opening of the heart-petals is the Nexus within and the connection with others through empathy is the Nexus outside us. "Wonderful!" she sighs.

For a timeless moment Sarah admires the petals in her hands and watches how they gently fall on the water. Then she walks along the edge of the stream, following the petals to their source.

"Muriel?"

Sarah goes pallid when she sees Muriel lying on the grass beside the stream, motionless. "That's it, she's gone!"

Panicked, Sarah runs to Muriel's side. A large basket of petals is turned on its side and the water is splashing the petals along, on their journey downstream.

"Oh Muriel!" Sarah cries, quickly holds Muriel's hand trying desperately to find her pulse.

"Help! Someone, help!" Sarah screams uncontrollably as her fitful tears fall.

"What's wrong?" Muriel asks, as she is startled into sitting up, wondering what all the fuss is about.

Sarah is so glad to see that Muriel is alive that she hugs and squeezes her.

"Sarah, I'm alright, there's nothing to worry about," Muriel reassures as she takes her straw hat and places it back on Sarah.

As Muriel grasps her gold locket to tuck back into her blouse, she explains to Sarah that she was collecting some petals but warmth of the sun invited her to take a nap. The stream seems to have taken all her petals.

Sarah shakes her head. "I couldn't find you for such a long time until I saw those petals in the stream. With their help, I found you. I was really worried. Don't you remember? We were supposed to meet for tea at ten o'clock."

"I'm so sorry," Muriel sighs. "I forgot all about it. I must be going senile."

"I looked everywhere for you. When I saw you just lying there motionless, I thought you'd died!" Sarah gently scolds.

"Oh Sarah," Muriel explains, embarrassed by the confusion, "I was just resting. I lost track of time. Even if I did pass away, it's alright, really, I'm at peace with myself and with my life, with God, with everyone. Everything is all right now that I've had my greatest wish come true."

"You're greatest wish?"

"Yes, you see, I want to be surrounded by love in my remaining time and your love for me became so clear now. That's what is most important to me, caring and sincerity, and the love shared between people. I'm content, and you are part of the reason why. Sarah you have a wonderful heart and I appreciate the way you have cared for me. Pierre and I regretted one thing in our life: We couldn't have children. You know, I feel close to you like you're the daughter I didn't have. Everyone at this retreat is like my family; this place is as Chandra said 'like a dream come true.'" Muriel stands and glances about with a thankful smile.

Sarah brushes the grass off her jeans and stands up beside her. "It's certainly beautiful, a real paradise" Sarah confirms while looking at the beauty of nature around them.

Together they walk, arm in arm, back to the stone house, in hopes of arriving in time for the afternoon discussion with Celeste.

Sarah and Muriel soon find themselves in the hallway of the old stone house. As they glance in the adjoining main room, they encounter a startling sight that leaves them wide-eyed in disbelief. There is Steven, the forty-five year old businessman, dancing with wild abandon all around the main room.

With his silver, balding head shaking rhythmically to the overpowering beat of rock music, Steven seductively unbuttons his one-hundred-dollar shirt, pulls it off and begins to swing it wildly above his head in dizzying circles. The music pounds, louder and louder. Steven next unzips his classy dress pants, moving his hips passionately to the rhythm of the music. His pants falling further and further down and he kicks them off, throwing his shirt into the distant corner.

"What are my eyes seeing?" Muriel inquires, placing one hand in front of Sarah's eyes. Muriel wants to keep her eyes closed but peeks out of one just to see the spectacle. "I don't think you should look, and neither should I," Muriel suggests finally closing her eyes tight.

"Oh nonsense!" Sarah laughs, pushing Muriel's hand away. "Who cares, I think it's hilarious."

"Look at that bright red bikini thong! That's all he's got on!" Sarah giggles in disbelief as Muriel opens her eyes.

They both laugh as they watch and wonder what in the world Steven is going to do next.

As Steven spins around, he catches sight of the two women laughing at his unexpected performance. "Funny? How about this?" Steven's dance becomes even more passionate and wild.

"Listen girls," he shouts over the music, "this is what it's all about."

"Dancing?" questions Muriel.

"Sure – it's all about having fun now, that's the only way to be happy," insists Steven between gyrations of his hips. "I've had enough of all this spiritual stuff. I can't see big money or profits in it for me."

After a couple of semi-disco moves, Stephen continues: "You know all of you could be right. I was too uptight – but not anymore…"

Celeste enters the room suddenly and abruptly turns off the music. "This is not up for discussion!" Celeste says with sincere concern. "Bring yourself together, so we can get on with today's discussion, which last I remember didn't involve vulgar dance moves. We're supposed to be starting. Steven, stop! Go in the back and put your clothes on and make yourself decent."

"Alright, alright," Steven mumbles, as he starts collecting his clothes.

Sarah yells out with a grin: "Oh! Don't make him stop. I wanted to see if that little red thong was also coming off."

Steven answers: "Hey, I did say I was letting loose!"

"Okay, that's enough!" Celeste exhorts. "We've had our fun but we're at a retreat not a striptease."

Once everything calms down and Steven is decent, Sarah asks Celeste: "Should I call Logan inside?" She noticed him sitting alone at a nearby picnic table looking blankly at the distant horizon in apparent melancholic contemplation.

"Let him be," Celeste insists. "If he wants to be with us he will do so of his own free will when he is ready. I feel that he needs space right now."

With that, Celeste lights a candle, while Logan sits alone outside — dejected and troubled, trying to figure out if he did the right thing in pushing away Sarah.

Celeste begins: "This guided meditation is the greatest journey that you'll ever take; it's the journey from your head to your heart."

Sarah catches one last flicker of the candle before she closes her eyes.

"Now take a full cleansing breath," Celeste instructs.

Sarah breathes deeply, and feels her whole body absorb the aromatics of lightly incensed air.

"Now," Celeste adds, "as you breathe out, let go completely."

Sarah releases her breath as she feels her entire body let go of all tensions.

"Make yourself comfortable," Celeste resumes. "Continue with slow, deep regular breaths. With each exhalation, relax more deeply. With each inhalation, imagine that you are breathing in aromatic incense with the power to fully relax while clarifying your mind..."

"Now we'll begin this once-secret and ancient practice," Celeste guides.

Sarah relaxes even further, enjoying the wonderfully uplifting sensations that fill her mind and body.

"Now visualize yourself standing in a forest clearing before a potter's studio. Look across to the mountains in the far distance. Imagine how it must be to gaze upon such a view in search of inspiration." Celeste elaborates as she continues to guide the group on their inner journey.

"Look about you, as there is no one to be seen. You draw closer to examine the tools and the finished examples of the potter's work which hang from the rafters."

Steven furtively peeks through his half-opened eyes in an attempt to analyze what the others are doing.

"The potter appears," Celeste intones, "and greets you as if he has been expecting you for some time. He offers to make a personalized amulet for you, something that symbolises your true inner nature and that will be uniquely yours. He looks at you with the eyes of someone who can see right through to your soul and then he makes a rough sketch of the design. What does he draw? Perhaps it is a symbol of your Higher Self, of your purpose in this life, or your particular strengths."

Muriel sits still, her body softly relaxed, her face content.

"Observe with interest as he then begins to place the clay amulet into the potter's stove, and closing the door the clay begins to cook in an intense heat," Celeste adds. "After a few moments he draws the clay from the fire and places it on his wooden bench. It cools in seconds. As you watch, he paints the clay symbol and carries it across to another bench with a pair of tongs. There, with his paintbrushes, he paints brilliant designs for a few moments, decorating the final shape until it's finished to his satisfaction. See the symbol, feel the heat of the stove, hear the potter's wheel turning, and smell the clay essence on the air."

Sarah enjoys this meditation with her senses fully engaged. She can easily envision every aspect of the journey.

"Finally," Celeste monotones, "he grips the amulet between a pair of tongs and plunges it into a bucket of water, filling the studio with steam. When the steam clears he takes it to his bench and attaches a small chain so that you can hang it around your neck. With pride he places it on your neck and now you can see it in detail. Take a long look at it and thank him for this gift."

For a moment, Muriel holds onto her gold locket that hangs from her necklace.

"Now imagine the scene fading as you feel yourself being drawn back into your body," Celeste instructs. "Become aware of your surroundings. When you are ready, open your eyes. Know that in subsequent meditations the gift you'll be given may alter. Perhaps it's a symbol of your current stage of awareness or something you need for the next phase of your life. It's yours to discover."

Sarah, Muriel and Steven open their eyes together.

"Not bad!" Steven laughs, surprised at how interesting the experience had been.

Sarah looks closely at Celeste. Celeste's face is unusually youthful for her age of fifty-eight. Her eyes are, as always, a vibrant, sparkling green. Her Rubenesque physique is relaxed and buoyant with a joyous and radiant facial expression. Celeste was born in India, as her parents had a deep interest in its history and were travelling there. She grew up in Vancouver and studied the violin there. She played professionally with many orchestras, performing extensively throughout the world. She met Chandra, her husband, in Vancouver. They wanted a quieter life, so they moved to Salt Spring Island, where they now live in retirement, which is an ideal place to pursue her interests of reading, gardening, cooking vegetarian meals, and occasionally composing classical music. Her marriage to Chandra is loving and harmonious. Once each year during the summer they would venture out to Elora to offer a retreat, with the intent of sharing inspiration with a small group of people who are guided to be there.

Celeste speaks with passion: "We're in turbulent times. So many old ways are disintegrating. Our old roles are vanishing. Out of necessity many of us must now invent the next steps of our lives. Over time, we must create a framework for ourselves with or without previous traditions for guidance. These traditions need to adapt to new social realties if they are to be relevant. Or, we have to invent new patterns. With development of new technologies, we constantly are required to keep pace with rapid changes. We're in search of ways to be well, to more fully understand our relationships and ourselves, as we look for meaning and a new centre of gravity within."

As the others contemplate her wisdom, Celeste continues: "Culturally, as a society we're in transition and beginning to awaken. New experiences and at times even stress triggers these awakenings. When we realize that a customary tradition has become blocked, or we notice that our anticipated roles just don't work, then we need to adapt. As a result, often life doesn't unfold in the ways that we had anticipated. We're in a world where the paradigm has shifted; the old and the new can often be found side-by-side. Yet the context and meaning of both old and new thinking has changed. So both of them have to adapt to current forces, otherwise they will become fossilized or dogmatic assertions without connection to human reality."

After a brief pause, Celeste notes: "The current reality calls upon us to be creative, and to find creative solutions. Ultimately we must look deeper within, and follow the heart. Some people will react to this by looking to what used to work, by reverting to old ways. However those ways cannot maintain distance from current changes. So the old ways will change and in some cases adapt."

"One aspect that has remained constant though is the search for the centre-point, the Nexus within us and which connects us to all of life," Celeste observes. "The journey to the Nexus is an individual path for each person. This path may involve discovering compassion, equanimity and courage. Sometimes it may necessitate a change in your environment instead of an inner transformation. When the change occurs, you'll find yourself at a new point, and feel a new connection to yourself and to all around you."

Logan dejectedly peeks through the window, hearing each word that Celeste speaks.

"You can compare this 'journey to the centre' to a wheel," Celeste advises. "Where the rim is your starting point, the spoke is your individual journey like individual spokes on a wheel, and the hub is the centre-point, the Nexus. The Nexus is your centre and simultaneously the heart of everyone. When you become consciously aware of it, then you connect to yourself and everyone else."

"At this point in time, our society is in the early stages of transition, so finding the centre has become even more important. Just think about our social institutions, political, medical, educational, economic, religious, and all throughout the work place and the family, all are undergoing significant change. What's the answer to finding one's way in the midst of all this change?" she asks aloud.

"The answer," she confirms, "is to be inspired, creative and heart-centred. Create new roles and patterns that work and are appropriate for our new times. We must learn to embrace change."

Meanwhile, outside, Logan feels alone, lost in his overpowering emotions of hopelessness and self-incrimination. How could he push Sarah away with such coldness? Why was he such a jerk? He could never forgive himself for his awful behaviour.

Inside: Sarah, Muriel and Steven listen intently as Celeste concludes: "This is the secret of all secrets! What is the bond, the connection between everyone here, between everything, everywhere in the entire creation? Listen as life speaks to you each day with the answers you need to hear. Look within to the still point to discover connectedness; find and live from your centre."

Steven inquisitively considers Celeste's words and asks, "Celeste, I wouldn't even know where to begin. Where do I start?"

"There are two main qualities needed to discover your centre," Celeste replies. "First is compassion, which involves connecting to the heart. Second is equanimity, which requires understanding and detaching ourselves from the reactive mind's flux of random thoughts and feelings, in order to experience even-mindedness in all conditions whether of joy or sorrow."

Steven appears to be reflecting on this message, as Celeste resumes speaking: "For most people compassion and equanimity are paths leading to the centre. For some individuals, their journey requires the path of finding courage within them, or creating the right environment outside them. It's only from that still point that solutions and wisdom are found. There is no power in a reactive mind, or in an isolated self. Remember compassion allows us to be conscious in the connection we seek. Equanimity allows us to connect to the truth within. Journey to your centre and create that connection."

Sarah smiles softly: "Celeste, I think in a small way I may have experienced a little of what you're talking about earlier today."

Celeste smiles and nods in acknowledgement, then continues: "Getting back to the wheel analogy: If your attention is focused outward it's like the outer part of the wheel where there's a lot of movement, chaos, activity. However, look inward and you can discover the centre of the wheel where you find true inner peace."

Muriel has a knowing expression and seems to understand. She is in full agreement with Celeste and happy that someone could express this wisdom so beautifully.

Sarah thinks that Celeste is deeply insightful and knows by direct experience that her understanding is deep and true. Sarah's only concern is that she has lost all sense of inner peace with Kurt. She is afraid that she has become overwhelmed with fear and turmoil.

Steven analyzes what Celeste said and questions the validity of it. *I'm just trying to do what works in my life,* he thinks to himself. Then, he asserts out loud: "All of this compassion and balanced mind philosophy will have to wait until I'm successfully set up in my next business venture. Then I'll consider it."

The discussion ends and Celeste suggests a leisurely stroll under the clear, starlit sky before retiring for the evening. As the group leaves the old stone building they stop to speak with Logan who is still sitting alone at the picnic table.

"Logan, you missed such a beautiful discussion and meditation this evening," Muriel declares as her warm eyes reflect sincere concern for Logan.

"None of this is working for me, Muriel. I came here to feel better. I'm not feeling any better. If anything I'm much worse now than ever. I've created my reality and I must live in it." Logan's tortured mind also reflects: *The problem is my own selfishness. So I hurt before I could be hurt. I feel awful for acting like an idiot.*

His outer and inner condemnations are interrupted by Muriel's words. "Logan, don't worry. Everything is going to be okay." Yet, her words are in vain, as Logan is lost in his guilt.

"Muriel, thank you for trying to encourage me but I need to be alone right now."

"Okay, Logan. If you want to talk anytime over coffee, just let me know."

Logan slowly disappears into the shadows of the woods.

As Muriel watches Logan leave, she's joined by Celeste and

Steven, who is still grappling with the evening's lesson. Steven asserts: "If I only had more money, I can then afford to be a better person."

"Steven look within your heart, and then you'll know what changes you need to make," Celeste encourages.

"Celeste," Steven counters, "many years ago I became disenchanted with people. I lost a close friend — no, he was more like a brother – because people didn't give money needed to save his life. Since then, I decided to put money first. I'll have you know, I never let go of my ideals. I just put them on standby until I could afford to be compassionate."

Celeste shakes her head. "Why wait? Live your ideals now! That perfect day to live them in the future may never come. I believe certain events can change us forever like the loss of your friend. Yet, have you made the best choice possible: To leave your ideals and just concentrate on accumulating wealth?"

"Of course it's the best choice," Steven snaps. "I've done what any intelligent person would do under the circumstances."

"Steven, in that very subtle act, you shifted out of your inner centre entirely. You chose to become money-centred instead of love-centred, which requires a compassionate heart at all times, whether in joy or sorrow, easy or difficult circumstances. The tragic loss of your friend doesn't prove that money is what matters. Actually, it shows the opposite."

"What do you mean?"

"Your friend had people around him who were wealthy. They could have helped but they chose not to help him. If these so-called friends responded with compassion they would have worked together to come up with the money to save his life. Lack of money didn't kill your friend, it was lack of compassion."

Steven's expression grows gravely serious as he senses that Celeste has given him another way of looking at the tragic loss of his friend. After a long pause, he speaks: "I never meant to become money-centred. Really, my desire for money was to support my ideals. The money was supposed to be the means not the end but somehow my priorities changed. I lost the clarity of my youth and I know I've hurt people along the way. I thought I couldn't afford to do anything else to survive and to get to the top.

Besides if the tables were turned they'd do the same to me in an instant. It's the law of the jungle that prevails: 'eat or be eaten.' The strong survive and the weak... well, they get stepped on."

"You may be right, Steven," Celeste considers. "In certain circles that may be the prevailing ethos, but a counter-ethos is also possible. That ethos proclaims compassion: Caring for the weak and frail members of society. Many of the great spiritual teachers, Christ, Buddha, Gandhi, Guru Nanak, have proclaimed it in their teachings. Rather than competition and looking out for number one, we can look out for each other with a caring heart. Instead of competitiveness, co-operation, I believe, works much better in many areas of life. In fact, I would argue that the real competition is with yourself: To be the best person you can be."

Steven becomes silent, reflecting on everything Celeste discussed. It was a new approach but he could see its benefits. He could also see that his life needed to somehow change. It couldn't be just about acquiring more and more wealth, especially at the expense of his personal values and ideals, which he is beginning to remember and regret losing.

Celeste motions Muriel and Sarah to also join her and Steven. When everyone gathers together, she states: "Self-development can occur in two distinct but mutually dependent areas: In the mind and in the heart. The mind needs to develop steadiness like the steady candle-flame mentioned before at the retreat. This equanimity or balance allows you to remain connected to your peaceful centre even in the midst of emotional and mental change. Along with the mental equipoise, the heart needs compassion. Compassion unlocks the heart's tenderness, empathy and understanding."

"Very interesting!" Sarah remarks. Then, she asks: "How are compassion and mental balance mutually dependent?"

Celeste smiles. "Just imagine a person who develops equanimity without compassion. That person would have great concentration but without the heart's compassion they would not have the guidance needed to use wisely their mental powers."

Steven responds: "You know I have scored high on IQ tests and I am in MENSA but I have stopped caring for people along the way."

"Well, Steven," Celeste offers, "the key to self-mastery is self-reflection. If you can see where you need to improve to create balance, then it's never too late to reclaim harmony in your life."

Celeste then adds: "You can also imagine a person with compassion who has a big heart but yet hasn't developed equanimity, so that his or her emotions and thoughts are all over the place. Just consider which you need to strengthen in your own life: Compassion of the heart or your mental equilibrium."

Logan, who is observing quietly from a hiding spot in the woods, realizes he has no problem with compassion but his emotional world and even his thoughts are in absolute chaos. He realises also that he can't even control his words and deeds, otherwise how could he be so unkind to Sarah? *But, it's too late now,* he thinks. *I've done great damage that can never be repaired.*

His thoughts are interrupted by Celeste's voice: "Before you leave, please look up into the sky. It's so clear. See the Big Dipper? Now follow along from the end of the Big Dipper to the next brightest star. There's the North Star. The North Star is the only star that doesn't move in the entire sky. All the rest of the many, many stars move you know. If you are ever lost, look for the North Star and then you can find your way, then you'll know what direction you're going in."

"Incredible. I never knew that," Sarah gazes in awe at the vast array of stars.

"You see," Celeste advises, "the truth is reflected everywhere; in the sky and also in each of us. In a sense you are the universe. Just as in the sky, with its wondrous North Star, each one of us also has a still point, that infinite centre of peace and wisdom; the point of stillness at the very centre of your heart. If ever you are troubled or lost the stars of the night-time sky will speak to you that there always exists a still point. Let that be your reminder to look within. Discover true inner peace and wisdom that gives the clarity that you may always know your way."

Sarah and Muriel thank Celeste for a great evening. Then, they walk away together. Steven remains behind, subdued, "Wow! You covered a lot today, Celeste. I have so many questions but I'll save them for tomorrow. You've given me so much to think about."

"I'm glad to hear that you benefited from our talk. Goodnight Steven!" Celeste chuckles, while remembering Steven's dance routine earlier that evening.

Steven begins walking toward the stream, keeping his eye on the North Star.

Celeste gazes out into the bushes where Logan thought he was well hidden: "Goodnight Logan! If there's anything I can ever do to help just ask. Remember, I'm here for you." She waits for a response and then she turns around looking up at the brilliant stars.

Logan remains quiet wanting the shadows to swallow him. Then, he looks away from Celeste and looks to the sky trying to locate the North Star.

When everyone had left, Logan stands alone, his black hair as dark as the night sky. With his sorrowful grey-blue eyes he once again gazes at the heavens. The stars don't change his sombre mood. He strokes his stubbly beard as he reminisces about a time when the stars were once little lights of inspiration, yet now they too appeared to him as if they had lost their glimmer.

Logan slouches as he begins walking back to his room.

He wants to sleep forever and to never wake up. Only then can he escape from his unbearable feeling of guilt.

Logan enters his cabin and pulls out his knapsack from under his bed. He rummages through it and confirms that his rope, previously hidden in the trunk of his car, is still there. He moans to himself, "I'm tired and I just want to die. Last time my attempt was pathetic but this time the rope will succeed where the pills failed." An owl hoots outside his cabin window, as Logan puts the rope back in his knapsack thinking that he heard someone outside. But it was just the wind.

In a sense you are the universe. Just as in the sky, with its wondrous North Star, each one of us also has a still point, that infinite centre of peace and wisdom; the point of stillness at the very centre of your heart. If ever you are troubled or lost the stars of the night-time sky will speak to you that there always exists a still point. Let that be your reminder to look within. Discover true inner peace and wisdom that gives the clarity that you may always know your way...

- Celeste

10

The Turning Point

Logan wants to be buried in the darkness around him — to bury his shame away from the light of day. He had hurt the woman he claimed to love so much. How could he do that? Now regret and guilt fill his heart to capacity with no room for hope, belief or love. He clearly recognizes now that he can't live without Sarah.

All this time he had longed to be with her. Then why did he push her away so easily? Since his talk with Chandra, he realizes his problem is not just depression rooted in chemical imbalance of the brain; rather its roots extend into a spiritual dimension.

He despaired over his loss, particularly the loss of his love. Before pushing Sarah away, his suffering was limited to melancholy, emptiness and hopelessness, but now, it extended into self-hatred and loathing borne out of guilt. He realized that he had an opportunity in his love to transcend his ego by releasing hurt, pain and anger. However, he decided to become ego-centered. So before he could be hurt again, he decided to exact revenge on Sarah and keep her from ever hurting him by striking first.

Logan's guilt is so suffocating now that any hope of progress is completely lost. He knows that he could never recover from it even with medication, self-help, or even with this retreat. He feels like a mouse spinning round and round within a glass ball with no chance of escape. The problem as Logan now sees it is self-evident: He had deluded himself. He had allowed hope to enter like a tiny candle whose feeble flame cannot match the might of the gale around it. Eventually, the candle's light will be snuffed out. It's just a matter of time. Even if the light survives for a time, its survival will be the cause of the candle's destruction. Either you choose to be snuffed out quickly, or you wait and wait until the wick of life is consumed.

Similarly, attachment brings in due course inevitable separation, isolation and death. The part within — that feels, that loves also gets destroyed with bitter experiences until finally love ceases as the heart stops feeling, surrounded in the vacuum of its meaningless nothingness. And, you turn away from life itself and take your final bow from the stage of life. So, you decide to no longer follow the script. Should hope exist when that hope's existence is but a moment in the field of time-space? Hope, in the final analysis, proves illusory as it can't survive long enough to create desired change.

Without hope, why even live at all, Logan wonders? He pulls out the rope, the noose from his knapsack and clutches it in his hands. *The answer lies here,* he thinks. *I have struggled long enough and now want to be done with the burden of living, especially to end pain and disappointment forever. To feel nothing would indeed be heaven.*

He ties the rope to a solid beam on the ceiling of his cabin. He can hear the rain hitting the cedar roof shakes as he steps onto a stool. In a moment, he would put the noose around his neck, kick the stool and with enough force downward his windpipe would be broken in an instant. So, he steps on the stool and holds the noose in his hand. Then, he hears Chandra's deep voice imploring: "Don't do it, Logan!"

Logan turns around and sees Chandra standing in front of him with brilliant orbs of red, yellow and blue. He looks the same as Logan's first vision of him in his dream. Even in his despair, Logan feels elated to see his wise teacher. But, he wonders if the Chandra before him is real or imagined.

"Logan, whether I'm physically here or a mental fabrication isn't important. I have come to appeal to the part of you that wants to live and love. The part of you that knows your journey can end here but it doesn't have to be so. Your decision is based on what you feel right now but feelings change. Remember they are like passing shadows of a cloud. Recognize the emotion, feel it fully, then let it go. Your life has a chance of getting better and I will help you get through this." As Logan ties the noose around his neck, Chandra implores: "Ending your life with this heavy consciousness and heart is not the answer, my friend. Please stop!"

"I don't disagree with you... but I can't go on!" Logan replies.

"I can only guess the pain you feel," Chandra intones. "But, your pain is not separate from mine. As a teacher, I feel your hurt, anguish and disappointment, yet I disagree with your abusive choice."

"Abusive? How is my choice abusive? I'm hurting no one."

"My friend, this is where you're wrong! You are hurting someone, someone very special and dear to me: A man by the name of Logan Andrews. You are about to commit violence on yourself. Any violence is mistaken and needs to be morally and spiritually avoided. Hurting yourself is just as vicious as injuring another person, especially when in time you can heal. You are also hurting those who love you. Please don't be rash. Stop, now!"

In response Logan places the noose around his neck and prepares to kick the stool.

Chandra pleads: "Before you go any further, I want you to answer one question for me: Why do you insist on hurting yourself? Why do feel compelled to commit suicide?"

"I think things are beyond talking and I won't answer you anymore," Logan replies. Now teetering on the stool, he adds: "This high stool can't remain stable any longer."

"It will remain stable so long as we communicate."

"I don't want to communicate!"

"Yes, you do!"

"How do you know what I want?"

"Because I am you."

"What? That's ludicrous."

"Don't you realize, my best friend, Logan? I am you. Look at me closely."

Logan closely examines but Chandra isn't there any more. Now, Sunny, the short man he met on his trek up the mountain, stands in his place. Sunny then transforms into Charlie, the building custodian for the newspaper where he worked. Bewildered, Logan shakes his head, as a frightening shape stands in Charlie's place now: The goddess without a face. He can hear her telepathically saying to him, "Your hurt is my hurt. Fear not, all will be overcome. Give life a chance. Believe, have faith and have courage." Then, she turns back into Sunny.

"W-w-what is going on?" Logan finally ventures to ask as he takes the rope off his neck. "Don't be frightened, my friend. All these faces you saw are guises that I have taken in my quest to help you."

"But, who are you?"

"Now, I had asked you that question when we met on the mountain top but since you ask it now, I will answer you. I am you. I am the part of you that wants to live, love and be fulfilled. So, when you are in need I have taken various forms by which to keep you from taking the wrong course of action. I am part of your imagination. The part of you that sees possibilities and hopes and that dares to dream. You have lost touch with me as you have yielded to negative, destructive thoughts and emotions. Yet, underneath all the darkness, I am still there like a small voice, a prompting and a yearning for wholeness. Do you still not recognize me?"

"I'm confused. Are you something I've conjured up all this time as Charlie, as the faceless Goddess or as you, Sunny?"

"If you want to look at it that way, then yes. Have you ever heard of the shape-shifters in stories?"

"Yeah, but that's only in folklore. It's not real."

"I am real, as real as your imagination. Do you doubt your imagination, your creativity?"

"I don't know what to think. I just go around in circles. Something is wrong with me but I can't see it. If you are me, then surely you must know what's wrong."

"Indeed, I do. But, I can't tell you, I will allow you to

experience it directly." Sunny walks over to Logan and waves his hand in front of Logan's eyes and exclaims: "Sleeeeeeeeeeeep, now!"

Those words act like a drug upon Logan's mind as he sinks into a deep stupor. When he is stirred, he is amazed to see his body glowing and even his face has an angelic radiance. He gazes at himself in a mirror. The image staring back is Sunny's. Somehow he has transformed into Sunny. He hears a whisper asking him to look closer. As he does, his face is slowly changing into his own but is lit with a heavenly glow. He finds himself dressed in a white robe and his face had a perfectly peaceful expression. He hears Sunny's voice speaking soothingly:

"This is the perfect you, Logan. It is your Higher Self: The part of you that knows not defeat, fear, anger or hatred. You radiate intuitive awareness, perfect belief and faith, and unconditional love and compassion in this higher state. You may forget but this state of being is your natural condition. Everything else is passing shadows, whose reality is conditional. So long as you remain unaware of your true nature — of who you really are, the shadows can cloud your mental and emotional state. Do you understand, Logan?"

Logan nods confidently in affirmation.

"Now, Logan, are you ready for the task at hand? Are you prepared to confront the shadows that cloud your mind and trouble your heart?"

Beaming with courage, Logan's voice booms with a roar that surprises him: "I am prepared for the struggle!"

"I know you are, though be aware that you may face your darkest shadows: Fear, hurt and anger. These three forces you have kept hidden, yet they trouble your mind and lead you away from mental balance, but they will come to the surface if you decide to persevere. Can you handle facing the shadows with the light of knowledge as your only weapon?"

"Yes!"

"Remember what three pillars support your knowledge?"

"Yes, intuitive awareness, perfect belief and faith, and love and compassion!" Logan thunderously proclaims.

With those words, utter darkness blankets Logan in a tight vice. It feels, as if he is suffocating under the weight of the darkness. He hears faint steps somewhere in the distance decisively approaching him but he can't see who it was.

His previous self-assurance surrenders to a tinge of fear as he asks: "W-who is there?"

Instead of a reply he hears shrieks and howls and then grim laughter. Logan's previous confidence starts to diminish as fear grips his thoughts. Who was out there, he wondered? Those shrieks and howls did not sound natural but fiendish. He now hears swift steps approaching. Then, he sees eyes glowing like red embers and white fangs that glisten in the oppressive murkiness. As his courage seeps away, Logan hears Sunny's voice: "Remember the Light that exists within your Self."

Those words reverberate in Logan's mind and with each echo his whole body glistens intensely with a feeling of balance and harmony. With the light, he sees the creature before him. It has sharp fangs, red eyes and a high forehead with sharp horns. As the light continues to increase, Logan can distinguish the shape of the face. It is clearly his own face but looking demonic.

The creature shrieks, "Surprise!" In an instant, it is on Logan trying to rip at his throat. But, Logan holds him at bay with his outstretched arms.

A wry smile appears upon the evil twin's face. He sarcastically adds: "You are pathetic! You can't defeat me! Then, he menacingly adds: "I am your shadow. I know all your fears."

Logan asserts: "Light will win over darkness."

The evil twin hollers with delight and tears at Logan's face with his claws, ripping through his skin as a knife cuts butter. Crimson trickles of blood spurt out and the malevolent twin sneers with euphoric delight. A ravenous gleam animates his eyes and he reveals ivory-white daggers ready to shred open tender flesh of his nemesis.

He bellows: "You are frightened!"

Logan's hands tremble with fear but he tries to hide it. He wonders at that moment, what frightens him? As death was his perverse attraction, why should it then terrify him now?

He realizes the fear was not death but pain. He is scared of pain. Physical pain on the surface level and below it the pain of loss — of losing his way in life. And, a greater pain remains below all these other hurts: The pain of separation. That hurt is like a leaf separated from the branch, knowing that it could never be reconnected.

Logan remembers that as a cameraman he filmed a refugee camp where children died every hour from hunger. Instead of feeling sorrow for their suffering, his primary interest was keeping the camera rolling, so that every cry, every tear could be recorded. His intentions were noble: To broadcast the misery, so that people would know about it and offer help. Yet, he felt hollow when he returned to his hotel that evening, as he realized that he treated the dying as a story and not as real people. That gap, that disconnection at the heart center was his greatest fear. That within him was a horrific beast that only pretended to care but could not really care.

"Logan!" his vile adversary shrieks. "Your fear fills your heart, for you are full of doubts. These teeth in a moment will sink into your flesh. When my canines rip open your jugular vein, what can save you then?"

Without realizing what he spoke, Logan intones as if speaking in a dream: "The Light of Knowledge is my only weapon!"

"The Light of Knowledge?" with a taunt the fallen self contemptuously mocks. "Logan you are living on the razor's edge and in a moment I will scratch your eyes out and devour you whole."

The creature exposes his fangs and dives straight for Logan, as fast as the wind. In a second, he claws at Logan scraping his tender flesh with his jagged claws. Logan screams in agony as the nails mark a stripe down his back and crimson rivulets flow freely drenching his previously white robe. Yet, he protectively keeps his hands around his neck, not exposing it for a moment.

"Why don't you give up?" The voice of his rival changes to a familiar voice from childhood: That of his father. "You are a pathetic coward! I can't stand the sight of you. That's why I left you and your mom! You are a complete failure! You are so afraid that you'd rather kill yourself, than face your doubts."

As he hears those words, something starts to change in Logan. At first, it is hardly noticeable. Then, it gains strength. He finds the reason his mind is troubled: His belief and faith were not perfect. With this knowledge, he stands up, ready to face his enemy assertively. Yet, his enemy is nowhere to be found. He has disappeared without a trace like a terrible nightmare that subsides with awakening consciousness. His heart feels triumph as if he has sublimated an inner demon, so that it can do no harm.

Then, from above a beam of light warms his face. Tears of joy run down his cheeks. He is free, free of the oppressive weight that clouded his thinking and crushed his hopes and dreams. At that moment, he knows that the dark thoughts that troubled him will never again spin out of control.

Sunny's voice is heard like a soft whisper: "Congratulations, Logan! You have overcome your fears with faith. Faith you thought you lacked – but you found it. You found it in your heart, which your mental fog made you to doubt. You have recovered the purity of your higher awareness, beyond the divisions imposed by the doubting mind. From now on you can trust yourself and reconnect to humanity, as you have reconnected to the source of mental balance within you. Go now, my friend, and live fully!"

11

The Trigger

A s Logan wakes up, his fingers move while grasping some cord-like object in his hand. He realises without even looking at it: The object is that awful noose. It is an abject reminder of his previous suicidal thoughts. Now he feels hope, which renews his faith and compassion. His spirit is rekindled with both courage and joy. While accusingly gazing at it, Logan is reminded for a moment of his melancholic existence in which suicide seemed a logical solution to his inner anguish. In contrast, his new-found belief gives him assurance that hopelessness and fear would never drive him away from life's challenges. From now on, his courage would stand resolute in any situation.

As he looks at the rope once more, resolution stirs his mind. After kindling the fireplace and as the flames arose, Logan rids himself of his burden. He tosses the noose into the fire and it is at once immolated. His face glows red with dancing shadows across it from the fire's flickering inferno. He is forever free of his self-destructive and fearful thoughts. He carried that rope so long and it was such a burden. Now his heart feels relief, for he no longer needs an exit strategy. He is determined to live life with intuitive awareness, right beliefs and a compassionate heart. He can feel that connection, the Nexus that Chandra and Celeste always mentioned, in his heart. Through his experience, he now also feels a connection to others, since through connecting to his inner self, he feels confident reaching out to others centered in inner harmony and peace. After a long time, he feels comfortable with himself and his life.

Gratitude for being alive arises in his heart spontaneously and a tear of joy trickles down his cheek. As Sunny had instructed him, Logan knows he would live fully now. Logan decides to go to Sarah and apologize to her for his abusive behaviour, for driving her out of his cabin in a fit of incensed rage.

Yet, anger still stirs his heart. He is angry at Sarah for having disappointed him, for having left him. *Maybe, it is too early to communicate with her,* he wonders? Logan thinks of the maxim: Time heals all wounds.

Logan decides to go for a walk and contemplate his next course of action. As he opens the door, Steven is waiting just outside with his hand raised.

"Oh, Logan! You saved me the trouble of knocking."

"Well, what brings you by, Steven?"

"I have something to share with you — a deep revelation. At least, I consider it deep."

Logan reflects how strange it is that Steven's revelation would coincide with his own expanded awareness.

"Oh, what's this revelation?"

"Before I explain the revelation, would you mind if I indulge in telling you a story."

"Sure. Lay it on me."

"You see, 20 years ago actually it's closer to 25 years now… I can't believe how quickly time passes — As I was saying 25 years ago, a young idealist boy, a flower child of the sixties, who was high on love among other things with his friends and his musical band, 'Incandescent Lotuses,' believed he could change the world with love and understanding."

"His best friend, Paul, who was not just a friend but more like a brother, was always beside him. A special bond existed between them. They did everything together from going to political and student rallies to playing music and going to hip parties. Their dream was to make it big as musicians. Strangely just at the start of their ascent to success, something terrible happened. A record executive had met them after a gig, expressing interest in signing their group to his label."

"Paul and his friend were ecstatic about the deal. It was their big break. After the good news, they were practicing some chords together for their upcoming recording session. When Paul reached for his coffee, he slumped forward and complained about feeling nauseated. Then, he fell from his chair and lay motionless in what was later determined to be a coma. He was rushed to the emergency. Tests revealed he had acute liver failure and required an urgent liver transplant."

The story mesmerizes Logan but he ventures to ask: "How does this story relate to your revelation?"

"Don't worry, Logan. I'll explain in a moment."

"Okay, I'm listening."

"When they got to the hospital, Paul's friend was told about the cost of the surgery. Paul and his best friend, who was if you didn't already guess it, none other than me, didn't have much aside from their creativity and music. So, I pursued every single person we knew to raise money to save Paul before it was too late. But, you know no one helped, even his wealthy friends and acquaintances refused to give money, and the record executives declined to pay anything up front."

Steven lets out a long sigh. "Without the needed money, I was helpless and within three days of being admitted to the hospital Paul died because he couldn't get the needed liver transplant."

"His death convinced me that my idealism was futile," Steven explains. "It suffocated my youthful creativity and desire to change the world. Whenever I thought of picking up the guitar to play music, I would remember Paul's face. How could I continue playing our music when he was gone?"

"He was gone forever because people didn't care. His death could have been avoided if people, especially those who claimed to be his friends, put his life before money. I felt powerless and I soon realised what matters in the world. Love, kindness and positive thoughts were useless. Power and control only rested in having money. The more money you have the more your influence," Steven concludes.

"So from then on, I changed my focus from changing the world through music to acquiring wealth. Eventually, my long hair yielded to a crew cut, and my faded jeans and tie-dye shirts changed to a suit and tie. I became the very thing I despised: a conservative prick. I became part of the establishment. At first, I justified my change as a means toward creating a more just world. Over time, money itself became the goal and my ideals were sold out. Even love didn't matter to me because I was blinded by an insatiable desire for control that I thought money gave me."

"Wow, remarkable story! So, losing Paul changed your whole life," Logan remarks.

Steven confirms: "Yeah, that's what started it. You see, he was more than a friend to me: I loved him like a brother and when he died, a part of me also died, the part of me that cared for people. I now realize why I closed my heart. I was afraid to reach out because if I became attached and lost another person I cared for, I don't know if I could take it. So, I subconsciously felt that money couldn't hurt me like an attachment to people. That's why I dedicated myself to acquiring more and more money."

"You tried to buy happiness, in a sense," Logan suggests.

"You know, Logan, I now understand back at that tender age, I could have travelled on two separate paths: One of love and the other of money. As I chose the second path, I lost the fulfillment gained from love and living from your highest ideals. Don't get me wrong, financial wealth is important, yet our life and relationships are more than just transactions. Running after money doesn't come before our intimate relationships."

"But it did for you?"

"Yes, it did. In a consumer culture, I realize now that we can lose sight of the importance of love, family and community. We forget to value relationships and also fail to recognize that certain ideals can never be bought and sold in the marketplace."

"You've now come to see things differently," Logan suggested.

Steven nodded agreement: "Chandra has encouraged me to change tracks and go back on the right path for me. He says it's never too late and I believe him. I can find more satisfaction in life. A satisfaction that arises from spiritual peace found in a compassionate heart. I have been guided not by compassion but by fears and insecurities, which I have tried to overcome with amassing as much money as I could. Yet, unless my heart changes and I put people first, which was my original intention, I realize now that I will *never* be satisfied."

"Wow, Steven, your journey has been amazing. I've gone through similar fears myself and like you I realize the dread of being hurt again kept me in a cocoon."

"Have you come out of your cocoon, Logan?"

"Mostly but I feel some metamorphosis still needs to occur."

"Well, maybe, I should explain something else to you then. When I felt Paul passing away, my strongest emotion was hurt and pain. In a few days, this hurt turned to anger. How could people not respond to him and let him die, even people that I thought were our friends? How could he be allowed to die in a hospital surrounded by doctors and nurses? Soon the hurt and anger dissipated and I intellectualized the whole event from a safe distance."

Steven paused at recalling the memory, then continued: "I developed a belief that equated attachment and love with weakness. I understood love as something, if allowed to enter the heart, would ultimately lead to pain and loss. Money, on the other hand, was benign as it offered safety and security. At first, I justified my change in values by insisting to myself that money was the means to achieve my ideals of justice yet eventually, without even my noticing, it became the goal for me. I became like the so-called friends who let Paul die, who placed money above everything else, even human life and compassion."

"Now, that you know all this. What are you going to do next, Steven?"

"I know exactly what I have to do next. I have to build creative space where music can come alive, especially for aspirating musicians with passion and idealism, and I owe a sincere apology to a woman who really loved me. It'll require a complete change in direction for me but I feel so alive right now. I wish I had realized all this sooner but it's never too late. So, I have come to say good-bye. I want you to also send my best wishes to everyone else, and tell Sarah that I apologize to her for my arrogant behaviour. I know it annoyed her many times."

"I promise to send your greetings to everyone and maybe you can apologize directly to Sarah later on. I also owe her apologies."

"You know, it takes courage to admit when you're wrong. When you do admit it, you stop punishing yourself." After taking a deep breath, Steven adds: "Well, I'm off!" as he stretches out his hand and gives Logan a hug. Then, he adds while warmly holding Logan's shoulder: "Take care, my friend."

"So long, Steven," Logan replies. He continues to watch him, as he becomes a distant figure until he can no longer see him. He wonders how Steven would transform his life and he feels glad to see the change in him. He knows he would miss his presence at the retreat, especially the competition between them in their meditation and yoga skills.

Logan reflects on their conversation, until he realizes his own despair was rooted in internalized anger. His anger was not at Sarah, instead his anger was like a collapsing star that turned its force within and it led to self-destructive thoughts and emotions. He had to rid himself of this anger before he could fully heal.

He remembers Chandra's words: "Forgiveness is the key." In that instant, in his heart he forgives himself for not being perfect and forgives everyone else who had ever hurt him unintentionally or intentionally. With that sincere forgiveness, his heart feels lighter and his mind is at peace. He would also ask for Sarah's forgiveness the next time he saw her.

Suddenly, as he turns around to head into his cabin, he hears a piercing shriek of a woman. Followed by the same voice calling his name "Logan, Logan!" at the top of her lungs.

Then, silence followed by a loud, echoing bang. It was a sound that at first he didn't recognize. Then, he remembered the time when he wandered in the woods as a boy. When he came to a clearing, he heard the report of a hunter's rifle going off and a deer falling with a thud in front of him. He tried to rescue the deer but it was too late. As he touched her cold body, the doe's eyes became cold and marbled as the life force was extinguished.

Logan didn't want anyone to get hurt at the retreat. So, his feet start carrying him in the direction of the report. He cuts through undergrowth and then he peers through bushes.

He sees Sarah stooped on the ground sobbing with a tall, clean-cut man standing imposingly above her with a handgun in his hand. He now holds the gun menacingly at Sarah's head.

The man roars acrimoniously, "If I can't have you, then no one else will!"

Sarah's heart is pounding as she waits for the bullet to go through her skull. She stammers, "Kurt, th-this is what you call love?"

"Yes, my love is unwavering. You have brought this upon yourself! You have betrayed me by running around and sleeping with another man. If he was here, I would put this bullet through his head first."

"I'm right here, Kurt," Logan announces as he comes out into open space and walks over to Kurt. Logan shouts: "Leave, Sarah alone! Your problem is with me!"

Kurt smiles. "This is better than I planned. I'll kill both of you. Neither you or she deserves to live."

Then, Kurt turns around to Sarah and adds: "I loved you, Sarah but you deceived me. You were unfaithful to me and I saw everything. You and Logan have committed sin, and so you both deserve death." He begins squeezing the trigger as Sarah closes her eyes in fear.

Logan implores: "Kurt, hold on. Stop! Love does not destroy. You can't call what you are doing love. It's pure anger, hate. You need to stop and listen to me."

"Go on, I'm listening," Kurt retorts, "but my decision is made. You have two minutes to speak."

"Before you say anything, Logan, let me talk to Kurt," Sarah interjects.

"Well, my little chickadee has decided to speak up," Kurt taunts.

"Yes, I have. I'm no longer afraid of you even if you're standing behind a gun."

"Really?

"I know underneath it all you're a coward."

Kurt's jaw tightens. "You'd better watch it, or else…"

"Or, else what? You claim to love me but you see me only as an object. Your love is nothing more than sick obsession. I'm tired of living in fear of you."

Kurt's face goes white with anger and the veins in his temples throbs. He prepares for retaliation, but this time Sarah doesn't cower. She loudly states, without fear: "You can't control me, Kurt! Do you hear me? You can kill me but you can't chain me anymore!"

"Shut up! Otherwise, Logan gets it!" he threateningly yells.

Sarah becomes quiet because she could face her own death; she had lived as a victim of threats, coercion and violence for so long that her life matters little to her. But, she does not want Logan to be harmed. She often thought that only by her death could she be free of Kurt. So, she was prepared for death but she was not prepared to see the person she loved become a victim of Kurt's violence. In a way, she blames herself. Destiny gave her Kurt because she did not remain steadfast to Logan.

"Logan, I'm a man of my word. I said I would give you two minutes. So, speak. You know I'm enjoying seeing both of you squirming. That's why I'm in no hurry but I can't take forever. I give you your two minutes starting now."

"Well, that's so generous of you. I get a full two minutes to speak while you threaten us with your revolver," Logan sarcastically remarks.

"I have to do what I have to do. Don't get all emotional like a woman," Kurt laughs as if he told a witty joke.

"And, what exactly are you doing?" Sarah asks bewildered.

"I'm keeping us together. You have been unfaithful but I will not let you go. I have to teach you how to respect a man."

"How can I possibly respect you? Just look at what you're doing and you've done to me in the past. If you really loved me, you wouldn't put me through such pain. Your love is just a twisted obsession. It's really all about control — controlling my heart, mind and body. If I allow your control, then ultimately I'll be defeated — a woman alive physically but dead in spirit. Is this what you want?"

"You're a typical woman: Full of emotions. How can I possibly take anything you say seriously?" Kurt taunts with a mocking smile.

Logan pleads: "Kurt, if you really love Sarah, then listen to her and let her go. In fact, I take her words very seriously, so I give my two minutes to Sarah and ask that you listen to her carefully."

"You're worse than a woman, Logan. In just a short time she has you whipped."

"I guess that would bother you wouldn't it, Kurt: For a woman and man to be equal in a relationship."

"I don't want to hear this garbage. Your two minutes are up and my finger is getting tired of keeping the trigger squeezed."

"Why don't you release it then and finish me once and for all?" Sarah prompts.

"I can't... I won't."

"Why not? What are you afraid of? You have already inflicted great pain on me. I have lived in fear of your threats. Do you remember the time you were cleaning your rifle and intimidated me? Do you recall what you said then?"

"I'm in control here, not you!"

"I ask you again: Do you remember your exact words?"

"Listen, my chickadee..."

"Stop calling me that! I don't want you to demean me or treat me as a possession."

"Oh, aren't we getting testy. I'm merely treating you how you deserve to be treated. You have brought this upon yourself. I am a man of my word and I don't make worthless threats, I make promises. When I was cleaning my gun, I had told you that I would come after you if you left me and I would kill you if you deceived me. So, I am carrying out my promise. Otherwise, it would be unethical of me: I would not be keeping my word. And, I'm a man of my word. You don't know how far I will go to keep you and how far I have already gone to keep you."

"What do you mean?" both Logan and Sarah ask simultaneously.

"Oh, isn't that romantic! You two are like one tongue in two bodies. It doesn't matter; you're soon going to die. So, I'll tell you my secret. Sarah, do you remember how you repeatedly wrote to Logan and called him? He never called or replied to your messages when he was tending to his mother in California. Remember?"

"Yeah, that's what broke my heart."

Logan replies perplexed, "I don't remember you calling or writing to me. I thought you were angry at me and so you kept quiet."

"That's not true! I wrote and called you many times and left you messages."

"What messages?" asks Logan.

"Messages that I left with your mother's nurse. What was her name?"

Kurt responds with a derisive smile, "Oh let me see… Ruby, wasn't it?"

"How did you know her name?" Sarah asks.

Kurt now laughs manically: "She was working for me. I got her a job at Logan's home and had her intercept all your phone calls and messages. It was a brilliant plan. Wouldn't you agree?"

Sarah goes pallid with the realization that Kurt is more sinister than she had ever imagined. His design becomes clearer to her. He had created the chasm between her and Logan. She asks tearfully: "How could you be so cruel and deceitful?"

"It was the only way you would forget about your dear Logan and give me a chance."

Logan speaks up: "Kurt, don't you see your whole relationship with Sarah is based on deception? Your actions are manipulative and abusive because if you really look inside your heart, you will see your relationship with her is not built upon love, it is based on control."

Kurt becomes enraged. He would rather destroy Sarah than admit defeat. So, Kurt aims the revolver at Sarah's heart and presses further on the trigger

Sarah asks: "Kurt, do you love me?"

Kurt looks puzzled but after some hesitation indignantly replies, "Of course, I do!"

"Did I ask you to do any of this? Do you think I enjoy physical and verbal abuse?"

Kurt is silent with furrowed brow, wondering where her questioning is leading. After some hesitation, he proclaims: "Well, you brought this on yourself. You've never been faithful and now I have the proof. I saw you and Logan getting cozy. But you forgot something Sarah: you're mine and you always will be. I would kill you before I let you go."

"Before I take you out, I want you to see your lovely Logan's head get blown off. That's what you deserve!" He points the revolver right at Logan's forehead.

Sarah yells, "Wait! Wait! Your problem is with me, not him. She steps in front of the aimed revolver and courageously asserts, "You'll have to kill me first."

Logan screams, "What are you doing? Step out the way! I can't live without you!"

Kurt is incensed by the love between them, so he pulls the trigger and simultaneously, Logan jumps through the air. He pushes Sarah out of harm's way.

The bullet rips through Logan's abdomen and blood oozes forth. His body falls to the ground with a thud. In a few minutes, his pale face takes on the mask of death. Afterwards, all the blood drains from his face and his body becomes rigid. Sarah weeps beside his body, seeking desperately to somehow revive him.

She frantically checks for a pulse... there is none. She checks his breath... no breath either. Then, she shrieks in such pain that Kurt is terrified. She screams while looking directly at him: "How could you do it, you monster!"

In that instant, she loses any fear of Kurt because without Logan she doesn't care if she lives or if she dies. The past year living with Kurt was hell, yet she always found hope in her dreams of meeting her real love, who in her heart she had never abandoned. She had lost hope at a vulnerable moment and Kurt took advantage of it by having Ruby intercept her messages. He then proceeded to plant ideas in her mind: Logan stopped loving her, he had found another woman in California and that's why he lost interest, and Ruby might be that woman. She didn't want to believe it but he never answered her calls, or returned her messages. Whenever she called, Ruby always answered. She spoke as if she was the lady of the house.

Sarah hated leaving Logan. If she could, she would have told him the truth afterwards when he came to her door after his absence in California. Yet, she knew about Kurt's violent potential and insane jealousy. So to protect Logan, she pushed him away. Her heart ached with desire for him, yet her intuition told her she had to disconnect. It was the only way to keep him safe.

Sarah walks up to Kurt holds out her hand with such confidence that he flinches for a moment. She directs, "Give me the gun, now!"

He had fired the shot to gain control, yet now his bravado seeps away, for he was afraid. In contrast, Sarah has no fears only sadness fills her heart, as Logan Andrews is no more. His predicament dawns on Kurt: He couldn't intimidate Sarah and he would spend time behind bars for Logan's murder. The police would lead him in handcuffs to jail. He couldn't spend time in jail.

Then, he looks at Sarah and she stands before him with such strength, without any fear of death, that he is petrified of her. He tosses the revolver into the stream near the swans that peacefully glide on the water, unaware of the human violence that surrounds them. In fear he runs away like a petrified animal through the woods, trying to escape from the consequences of his crime.

Sarah walks up to Logan's lifeless corpse. A tear wells up in her eyes, which falls down on his cheek. She wipes it from his pallid cheek and kisses him, yet his lips are cold, without any sensation. They can no longer return sweet kisses. Sarah sobs uncontrollably, not knowing how she will ever survive this tragic loss.

12
Transformations

Three months had passed since the conclusion of the retreat. Sarah hears an angelic voice telepathically speaking to her: *Oh, child! You suffer greatly and I know the pain you carry in your heart. Now, it's over. You are in heaven now and you are united with your love.*

Sarah looks all around her without seeing with her eyes, yet her mind's eye can see it all. Heaven, a place that no eye can describe, no human ear can narrate its harmony, and no human heart can convey its perception. What she sees is beyond her imagination.

Everything including her body seems of a finer essence than physical existence like the difference between the materiality of solid objects and the subtleness of thoughts. She realizes she feels no inflow or outflow of her breath, nor does she perceive her heartbeat. The realization is disconcerting, yet her light-body, which isn't even really a body but a beam of energetic light in human shape, vibrates with peaceful silence, calmness and splendid brilliance.

Sarah realizes she must have died. The thought of being separated from Logan is too much for her. The angelic voice speaks again: *Your Logan is here and you are united with him. Just think about him and he is with you, for time and space are mere concepts here. Our reality is outside them. Everything is in the now. Hence, your imagination can make anything possible. Merely imagine or utter it and it will be. This realm is even subtler than your thoughts on earth. Think of him now and he is by your side.*

She imagines Logan with her full attention and in a moment she feels his warm hand on her shoulder. He utters: "Oh Sarah! How I've missed you!"

"I have also missed you," Sarah confides. "yet incredibly you are here in heaven with me. I don't know how but right now I don't care. I'm just glad we're not separated."

They kiss and it is unlike any kiss, for it creates total ecstasy in the spirit. That feeling stays forever with them only becoming heightened with each kiss. Hence, you can linger in the wonderful closeness and bond, rather than the ecstasy remaining encased in periodic moments of joy that are stolen all too quickly.

The angelic voice speaks yet again: *You two are soul-mates and whether distant or near will always be connected at the heart. Your relationship has a beautiful romantic side and beyond that its purpose lies in spiritual growth. You eternally remain spiritually connected forever. Yet, growth requires patience, fortitude and change. The road can be difficult, still tread it with love. The love you feel for one another is only one piece of the puzzle, though it is an important piece.*

"What else is there?" Sarah asks perplexed.

There is more, much more. Reflect on your life and the relationships in it.

As Sarah reflects on her life, she remembers Kurt. He held the revolver and then fired it into Logan's interceding body. She notices Kurt's great anger but then she feels his deeper feelings. Underneath the anger is real fear: Fear of being alone, fear of losing control and power, and his strongest fear, someone realizing that underneath his rage, he is only terrified and weak. In that moment, all the abuse and pain, she had experienced due to him is totally gone. Her empathy, her connection to his underlying feelings releases her from her fear of him forever. She no longer perceives him as a monster but as a man scared of life and turning to violence to hide his vulnerability. In that instant, she experiences myriad emotions originating from the earth. She intensely feels the joy of two lovers holding hands in a park, the fear of a spider as it is crushed under a newspaper, the pain of drivers and their passengers as their vehicles collide, and the wonder of parents beholding their newborn child in the maternity ward.

Sarah feels that her heart will explode from overwhelming compassion. As Logan touches her hair, emotions become calmed and intense with love, compassion, devotion, acceptance and a complete sense of comfort. Then, she knows she isn't meant to understand it all. She exclaims: "I heard their thoughts and felt their emotions. I felt an emotional connection to everyone. We are all interconnected!"

Love and compassion are the most important in life, my dear, the angelic voice whispers. *The whole is in the parts and the parts are in the whole. The entire universe vibrates as one. Sarah the love you feel, the love you give, the love expressed in thoughts, words and deeds is the most important. So now you must return to earth.*

"I don't want to be without Logan! Wait! Wait!" she cries.

****

Sarah feels someone shaking her body, she hears her heart beating loudly and her breathing is heavy. She hears a familiar voice asking, "What's wrong Sarah? Are you okay?" It's Logan's wonderful voice. She isn't in heaven anymore but back on earth. Was it all a dream? No, the experience was vastly differently than most dreams and at the same time tragic with the loss of Logan.

Sarah exclaims, "Oh, Logan, I had an upsetting vision!"

"What happened?"

"I was in heaven, at least it seemed like heaven, and you were there too."

"Really? That sounds beautiful!"

"No, it wasn't! You stayed there but I had to return to earth. I almost lost you once and I'm not ready to lose you again."

"I know," Logan solemnly says. Then, he remembers his struggle to recover from the gunshot wound. He was taken for dead even when the paramedics arrived. Only later en route to the hospital did his vital signs return. Sarah was there with him, still hoping that he would recover. His breathing had been so faint that no one could see it or feel it. He had a near-death experience, which he didn't remember fully except for going into a peaceful light, connecting with his mother's spirit.

His mother had told him they would reunite when the time was right and that time was not now. He was enveloped by sheer peace, comfort, joy, and oneness with the entire universe. His heart felt such comfort that he did not want to return to the suffering world with its sorrows and pains. Yet at that very moment, he fondly remembered Sarah and in an instant he connected with her pain. He could hear her sobs, feel the pain of her tears, and feel the anguish of her loss as she cried over his body. If he didn't return soon, it would become a corpse. How could he leave her?

Logan knew he must return and he realized then that life is really about relationships, about intimate connections. Life cannot be lived free from sorrow, pain and loss. He could not escape from the tragedies in life, yet with an open heart he could reach out with love.

The love he and Sarah shared would always be expansive, warm and inspirational. The afterlife could wait for he wished to experience love and connection on earth. He resolved to embrace her and the love between them. Then he returned — returned to his body because of his love for Sarah

With their shared experiences, they know as they look into each other's eyes that they are meant to be together. They are fulfilling some higher purpose together. What that exact purpose is, they aren't certain but they *are* certain time will reveal it. Their experience with near-death and envisioned death make them certain that their love has a deep spiritual purpose and kinship. They hold each other lovingly in an eternal embrace and Logan whispers: "I want to marry you and to grow together in love, so long as we both shall breathe."

"I want that too and not only for as long as we breathe but even after!" Sarah delightfully replies. Before they can continue in their joy, she suddenly feels a sadness envelop her. She looks at Logan and his eyes reveal that he also senses it. Muriel has died!

Sarah remembers the phone call with Celeste:

"How are you and Chandra doing?"

"Oh, we are well! We have been home on Salt Spring Island for the past three months living peacefully close to nature. Chandra is really feeling connected to the natural beauty and the friends we have here. It's all about love for what you do and for the people around you."

"Logan and I realize that more than ever."

"I'm glad to hear that," Celeste says. Then after a pause, she adds: "Sarah, I have some sad news to give you. Muriel had struggled for the past three months but now she is nearing the end."

"Oh, no!" Sarah cries. Then, as she feels great empathy, she continues: "I won't let her die alone. Logan and I will go to her."

"That's so beautiful! The retreat has created some wonderful bonds. You know, Sarah, she's not alone."

"Who is with her?"

"Steven."

"Steven?"

"Yes, he left a young assistant to run his independent music label, which encourages young musicians with passion and a message to find an audience, in order to be with Muriel. He felt wonderful with this project but his priorities are now to put people first. So he left everything to support Muriel."

As she reflects on the conversation, Sarah is still amazed by Steven's compassion and she feels a great respect for him. Suddenly, the phone rings.

"I'll get it," Logan says.

It's Steven. He informs Logan: "Logan, Muriel died just a short while ago. She wanted you and Sarah to know that she wished you well. She told me that you and Sarah have a real connection like the connection Pierre and her shared. After the retreat, she desired more than anything to see Pierre in heaven. So, this wintry evening when the snow appears blue under the moonlight, Muriel breathed her last breath, she clutched Pierre's locket to her heart, and with her other hand held my hand. I felt very sad to see her go, yet her face looked so splendid that it gave me great comfort."

Steven continues after a period of tears: "Since she had no family, she gave Sarah all her money. I will have it sent to you according to her wishes."

"You are truly remarkable, Steven!" Logan replies as he reflects how Steven has grown in empathy.

"Well, I'd better get going," Steven says, his voice shaking. "I have many arrangements to make but I'll keep you informed, my friend."

"Thank you, Steven."

When Logan is off the phone and he tells Sarah the sad news, she remarks: "She must have passed away when we both felt it."

"Yes, our experiences are showing us that a connection exists between people we care about and us. When we feel great empathy and compassion, the Nexus within us is awakened. Through our sincere emotions with other people we create a connection, a Nexus, with others. That's the essential message we have been given ever since the start of the retreat and it was amplified with our after-life experiences. Now, with Muriel gone is the fabric of our connection, our Nexus, with her broken?"

"No," Sarah answers. "She is with us always as a living memory and I sense that our connection with her exists, yet it has changed."

Logan hugs her and kisses her, "You *are* amazing."

"We need to put these insights on paper in our writing."

"We moved back to our hometown to write and now you and I have a mission to share our insights with others and make them aware of the Nexus."

"Yes, very much so!"

The sun sets on wintry landscape outside as the two lovers sit bundled together in front of the crackling fire. They hold each other with total love, passion and affection. Their kiss feels like an elixir and it excites their passions. Both lovers feel an overwhelming shift in the energy at their heart centre, the petals of their hearts are totally open now. Fear completely melts away, as they could really feel a rush of the flowing energy of love and compassion between them. From that point on they were ready to openly embrace a direct experience of love in their life without any inhibition and in complete freedom, since they both were ready to give and receive love. The heart centre needed to be fully opened it seemed to overcome the block that prevented the flow of energy by a presence of fear and lack of confidence.

All hurts completely vanish now, and love flowers in their hearts. So, they passionately embrace with rapturous joy and their bodies move in unison to their sensual delight. Their energies and whole being are united as one. They are two bodies but one spirit, different yet so alike. The love and connection between them would always guide them in their life's journey together.

For those interested in attaining further spiritual enlightenment, the authors recommend getting to know the following books:

READING LIST:

Bach, Richard. *Jonathan Livingston Seagull*. Scribner: New York, 2006.

Bennett-Goleman, Tara. *Emotional Alchemy: How the Mind Can Heal the Heart*. Harmony Books: 2001.

Blake, William. *Songs of Innocence and Songs of Experience*. Dover Publications: New York, 1992.

Burns, David D. *The Feel Good Handbook*. New York: Plume, 1999.

Chopra, Deepak. *The Path to Love: Spiritual Strategies for Healing*. Three Rivers Press: New York, 1998.

Coelho, Paulo. *The Alchemist: A Fable About Following Your Dream*. San Francisco: Harper San Francisco, 1995.

Dyer, Wayne. *The Power of Intention*. Hay House: Carlsbad, CA, 2004.

Gawain, Shakti. *Living In The Light: A Guide to Personal and Planetary Transformation*. New World Library: Novato, CA, 1993.

Gibran, Kahlil. *The Prophet*. New York: Alfred A Knopf, 1923.

Kornfield, Jack. *A Path With Heart: A Guide Through the Perils and Promises of Spiritual Life*. New York: Bantam Books, 1995.

Millman, Dan. *Way of the Peaceful Warrior: A Book That Changes Lives*. New World Library: Novato, CA, 2000.

Moore, Thomas, *Dark Nights of the Soul*. Gotham: New York 2005.

Morrison, Deborah. *Mystical Poetry*, Manor House Publishing: Ancaster, ON,   2000.

Redfield, James, *The Celestine Prophecy*. New York: Warner Books, 1995.

Ruiz, Don Miguel. *The Four Arrangements: A Practical Guide to Personal Freedom*. Amber-Allen Publishing: San Rafael, 1997.

Sharma, Robin S. *The Monk Who Sold His Ferrari*. Harper: San Francisco, 1999.

Singh, Tara. *Gift For All Mankind*. New York: Ballantine Books, 1993.

Tolle, Eckhart. *The Power of Now: A Guide to Spiritual Enlightenment*. New World Library: Novato, CA, 1999.

Tzu, Lao. *Tao Te Ching*. Toronto: Frances Lincoln, 1999.

Williamson, Marianne. *A Return to Love: Reflections on the Principles of "A Course in Miracles"*. Harper Collins: New York, 1996.

Zukav, Gary. *Soul Stories*. New York: Free Press/Fireside, 2000.

Manor House Publishing Inc.
www.manor-house.biz
905-648-2193